FABULOUS TERRIBLE™

The Adventures of You™

FABULOUS TERRIBLE™

The Adventures of You™

Sophie Talbot

CHOOSECO
WAITSFIELD, VERMONT

Cover Design: Dot Greene, Greene Dot Design
Cover Photograph: Copyright Westend 61 Photography/Veer
Crest Graphic: Jenny Soloman/Crestock
Book Design: Stacey Boyd, Big Eyedea Visual Design

For information regarding permission, write to:

CHOOSECO

P.O. Box 46
Waitsfield, Vermont 05673
www.cyoa.com

ISBN-13: 978-1-933390-76-5
ISBN-10: 1-933390-76-X

Published simultaneously in the United States and Canada
Printed in Canada

0 9 8 7 6 5 4 3 2 1

For Jenny Paul, In Memory

Special acknowledgment to
Nicki Renna for her writing help.

"A girl should be two things: classy, and fabulous."
— Coco Chanel

All changed, changed utterly;
A terrible beauty is born.
— W. B. Yeats, Easter 1916

You press your hands firmly against the frosty glass window, and stare in at the rows of big plastic buckets filled with vibrantly colored ice cream. 129 flavors in all.

Like everything else in Hatterly, South Carolina, Ice Cream Dreamz started out quaint and quiet. But when Baskin Robbins moved in up the street, the owners faced their big chain bully head on: they installed flat screens, pumped in loud music, and hosted The Hatterly One-Hundred, a contest to name and create that many new flavors. In the end, afraid to offend a single potential customer, they made every entry a winner. A whopping 107 new flavors were born and branded, including the one by your 9-year-old foster brother Mason, oh so humbly named "Mason's Masterpiece." It consisted of vanilla ice cream with chunks of white chocolate, coconut shavings, and white sprinkles.

"Momeeee!" Mason whines on cue. "I want my ice creeeem nooowww!"

"Hang on, Pumpkin," your foster mom Karen pleads to her son. "Just a few more seconds. Those other people were ahead of us in line."

One look at Karen's platinum blonde hair, pallid complexion, and whitewashed, shabby chic, spotless, colorless, odorless home, and it's pretty easy to figure out who was the real "mastermind" behind Mason's winning flavor. She's not a germa-phobe or anything, she just likes things to be neat and orderly. "Everything has a place," Karen always says, and she has no problem telling you where it is as long as you put the thing there, the right way, of course.

While he stops complaining momentarily, Mason continues to moan.

"Mommmmmmeeeeeeee," he simpers.

You gotta give it to him, he's good. You were halfway to the mall when Mason managed to throw a screech fest so nasty that Karen immediately diverted the family SUV, and steered straight for the one place – the only place – that sells his kryptonite by the cone.

Mason didn't start out this spoiled or rotten. He was hit by a car when he was three, and...wait for it...Karen was behind the wheel! She didn't mean to hit her own kid, of course. It was one of those horrible accidents that happen in the blink of an eye. Karen was backing out of the driveway and thought Mason had gone inside with the babysitter. The babysitter thought he was with Karen. You know the story.

Miraculously, he turned out okay, suffering a minor concussion and some scrapes that healed up without a trace. Karen, on the other hand, was permanently scarred by the incident. Now she doesn't let him leave her side. Karen's guilt about the accident crippled her ability to say no, even when Mason is bad. Like a little genie in a bottle, all he has to do is rub Karen the wrong way and his every wish is her command.

Like today. It was supposed to be girls' day out, last minute errands before you left for school and for good. But then Mason whimpered that he wanted to come and *poof!* he got his wish. Karen could have left Mason at home with David, your foster dad, who is working in his garage like he does every Saturday afternoon. David is a really nice man who works hard, loves his family, and likes to be told what to do — so it makes sense that he married Karen, because she's really good at that. He doesn't mind running to the grocery store late at night for something Karen forgot but can't live without (like bleaching strips or fat free mayo), or planting a new row of pansies on a Sunday morning after church. He'll do all the "honey-do's" she can dream up as long as he's left alone for a few precious hours of "David Time" every Saturday.

"Which flavor are you feelin' today?" the college kid behind the counter shouts enthusiastically over the latest Avril Lavigne single blasting through the sound system.

You snap out of your own little ice cream dream and peel your numbed hands off the glass.

"Metaphorically speaking, I'm Rocky Road, but in reality, lactose intolerant, so nothing for me, thanks. Just give that kid over there his cone? So we can get back on the yellow brick road..."

He cocks his head, gives Mason a quick glance, then winks at you and cruises down the counter, head bobbing to the music. This guy gets it. He's kind of cute, too, like a less GQ version of Jake Gyllenhaal, and with a much smaller head. Could he be the one? His lips look a little chapped. Otherwise, he's got rhythm, clear skin, nice hands, good bone structure. Just as you're imagining what it would be like to plant one on him, he glances over at you and catches you staring. You pretend to be engrossed in the sign posted over his head explaining the nutritional contents of ice cream. This happens a lot lately – you imagining kissing random guys, and then getting caught in some embarrassing moment. Ever since your best friend Emily wrote to you from sleepover camp last month giving you the juicy details of her first kiss, you've become obsessed with procuring yours.

Luckily, Ice Cream Guy gets distracted when Karen empties the contents of her tote bag onto the counter in search of her frequent buyer card. Three lipsticks, a tube of breath mints, and a tampon roll off the counter and onto the floor by his feet. He fumbles to collect all but one lipstick, which he has to get down on his hands and knees to search for under the milkshake machine. Mortifying. And a total buzzkill for your fantasy kiss.

"Go find us a table, will you, sweetie?" Karen pleads to you as Mason clings to her leg yelling, "I want my ice cream NOW!" You wander past the discarded spoon bucket…gross…and take a seat by the door. The tiny bells above the door jingle as a slow paced pack of Senior citizens hobble in. That's when it happens.

It always starts the same way: a gentle tingling that begins in your feet and slowly creeps up your legs. Your face feels flushed. Your palms grow hot, even though they were freezing moments before. The noises in the room become a muffled echo, as if you're underwater. And finally the shimmer itself: a hazy image that glimmers around the edges, like a movie playing in your head.

Some would call it a gift, but to you it's a curse. You never know when you're going to shimmer, how long it will last, or what you'll see. But what you do know is that some time in the following days/weeks/months, the shimmer will come true.

Shimmers, you see, tell the future.

This one is extra weird.

A thick stack of aged paper sits on a tabletop. The once white sheets have turned a faded umber tinged with brown spots. The edges are tattered from being fingered and turned and the spine is curling from exposure to moisture in the air. A woman's hand puts a radiant gold fountain pen to the page and begins to write. The ink sparkles as though it is mixed with stardust that bleeds into the fibers of the paper like little sunbeams forming a halo around each letter. Her handwriting loops and curves slowly, but her palm is blocking the word she is forming. Just as you are about to see the first letter....

"You ready to go?" Karen suddenly asks. The ice cream shop begins to come back. The shimmer fades. You're looking at Mason sitting smugly next to his mom, slurping up the last bits of coconut and sprinkles from his cone. Your shimmer must have lasted a couple of minutes.

"Sure," you say brightly, standing up. You look around. No one is staring, pointing at you, or whispering. No one is even looking in your direction. Good, no one noticed.

"Okay, then," Karen says. "Time to do some serious shopping." You force a big smile and nod.

Back at home that evening, you stand in your room and stare at the contents of a large Macy's bag dumped out on your bed. You can't believe your eyes. The underwear Karen got for you are so not cool. First of all, they are cotton. Boring old cotton. And second, they're pink, lavender, and blue with little white flowers. That's right, flowers, people!

"Oh, they are so shabby chic!" she squealed when she saw them.

Shabby, yes. Chic, not so much. But they were on clearance, a feature that immediately makes Karen want to buy something, at least when it comes to you. It's not that you're not grateful. You are. But you were hoping for something a little less American Girl and little more Girls Next Door. You're about to go to Trumbull Woodhouse, one of the "Ten Best Boarding Schools" in the country and the only all-girls school on the list. Trumbull Woodhouse, where they're rolling in it.

Seriously, the school catalog looked like a Ralph Lauren ad, for God's sake. Those girls are probably going to have designer sheets and the satin underwear to go with them, like some Victoria's Secret catalogue shoot. And there you'll be, in your shabby granny panties. Great. You couldn't be any less cool if you tried. But then again, you've never been one of the cool kids.

You cross over to your full-length mirror and check yourself out. Luckily, a fourteen-year-old orphan who occasionally flies the freak flag in a big way can throw on some knock-off designer jeans, espadrilles from the Gap, and a hoodie and blend in with all the other girls her age. And you are all about blending in. As a foster kid, you've learned to keep your eyes open and your mouth shut. No complaining, no fighting, and whatever you do, don't rock the boat, cause if you fall into the dark, murky water, there is no one to save you.

Okay, maybe that's a little heavy for packing on a Thursday night, you think. Save it for your journal, sister.

Later that night, after you've scrubbed your face with the new alpha-hydroxy soap Karen got you that feels like you're rubbing Icy Hot on your cheeks, you lie in bed and think. This is your favorite time and place to go over things and make your lists. Lists help pull things together, put them in order, and make them make sense. It's the only way you can calm down and enjoy the peace and quiet.

Tonight, you wonder about where you're going and where you've been. You have no clue what these other girls will be like at your new school, but you're almost positive none of them will have a story like you do.

#1 You don't know who your mother and father are. You don't even know if they are even dead or alive.

#2 Someone left you off at an orphanage when you were

three months old. In a basket!

#3 You have no relatives that you know of. And if you do, what really sucks is that the sympathetic State of South Carolina won't let you learn about them until you turn eighteen. In the meantime, what do they expect you to do:

- just not think about it,
- figure things out on your own,
- or use your imagination?

Well here's a newsflash for them — that's exactly what you've done. You've lived in two state run girls' homes and three foster homes, located in four different cities. The Donovans were your third family, and you were hoping your last. Karen always wanted a daughter, but couldn't have kids after Mason was born. It was some kind of birth complication.

Things were great when you first came to live with them. They converted Karen's scrap-booking room into a bedroom, the first time you've ever had your own. Karen is a pretty good cook. She was really cool about showing you what to do and talking to you about your body when you got your period for the first time last year. David is always home in time for dinner and tries to help you with homework, even though he usually just ends up watching. But right after your thirteenth birthday, everything changed. That's when the shimmering started again.

You have a few memories of shimmering when you were little. You saw the mailman's lottery win four months before it happened. Ralphie Teener broke his leg falling off the jungle gym exactly five days after you saw it in a shimmer. That was back when you thought everyone got them, these little visions of the future. Then one day when you were about six or seven, an older couple came to the girls' home where you were living and took you to McDonald's for lunch. They let you order whatever you wanted, so of course you opted for the happiest meal on the menu.

You'll never forget that the little prize inside the box was a miniature, plastic Dalmatian from the Disney movie that had just come out. Then they took you to the park, played hide and go seek with you, and bought you an ice cream. The man wore a thick blue sweater and glasses, and she smelled like lavender. You accidentally got some ice cream on his sleeve, but he didn't seem to notice. They were too busy asking you if you wanted to come live with them. Although you had just met them, you remember thinking: you got to eat a cheeseburger, get a new toy, have some ice cream, and go extra high on the swing set all in the same day with them, so you said yes. Dude, if you ask a child a serious question, you're gonna get some serious child logic, what do you expect?

"We're gonna come back tomorrow and take you home with us, okay? Would you like that? To come live with us?" the man asked in the car on the way back.

Not have to go back to the lumpy bed and lumpier mashed potatoes at the girls' home? 'Mister, how fast can this thing go?' you wanted to say.

For the rest of the ride, you told them about your shimmers. Their eyes darted from you to each other, and it looked like it hurt their faces to smile. But all they said was, "what an active imagination you have." The next morning, you woke up and packed your little suitcase, shoved the Dalmatian in your pocket and waited, but…they didn't come. Anita, the house-mom, made you unpack your suitcase that night, but when you got up the next morning, you repacked it and waited again. They still didn't come. You packed and unpacked your bag everyday for three weeks until finally, you gave up and chucked that damn little dog into the trash.

One of the kids in the room next to yours said you must've done something or said something to make them not want you. At first, the only thing you could think of was the ice cream stain, so you vowed never to eat ice cream again. But later that night, while you were lying in bed, you remembered the funny looks on their faces when you described your shimmers, and you realized you couldn't tell anyone about them again. You also decided to put an end to these stupid pictures in your head.

The first vow was easy to keep, no ice cream. The shimmers were harder to control. When a shimmer came on, you did whatever it took to stop it: shook your head, screamed out loud, clapped your hands, rubbed your feet, turned on loud music, anything to distract you and snap you out of it. And while those things worked to drive the freak flashes off, that kind of behavior didn't fly with the other kids your age or your first two foster families. You were labeled a "problem child."

Over the next two years, you were poked, prodded, and pointed at by doctors, teachers, and the other kids around you. Funny thing was, all your tests were normal. Go figure, right? Eventually they stopped looking, and lucky for you, the shimmers stopped coming. That's when the Donovans came into the picture, and it felt like you finally had a shot at a normal life.

Or so you thought, my pretty...

Fast forward to your thirteenth birthday last year. Karen worked for three days straight to transform the backyard into a full Hawaiian beach blowout. David and Mason were recruited to hand the guests fruity drinks in coconut shells with little paper umbrellas. Kids from the neighborhood who you ride bikes with, a few girls from your soccer team, and your best friend, Emily, who's in your class, came ready to party.

You posed for funny pictures with your friends on David's old surf board as though you were catching huge waves in the middle of the ocean, played water balloon volleyball, and made paper leis. Later that afternoon, you sat at the head of the picnic table with all your friends and family gathered around you singing Happy Birthday. Karen made your favorite red velvet birthday cake in the shape of a whale. She set it in front of you ablaze with 13 candles.

You've always found blowing out the candles a little awkward. You don't like being the center of attention. Everyone looking at you, smiling and singing, makes you want to crawl into a hole or at least under the table. But you forced yourself to stay above ground and stare at your cake. Then, right at that moment, the familiar tingling started in your feet. You shifted a little on the bench seat. It had been a while, so you were hoping it would go away. But when it started to spread higher and higher, and you felt the heat in your hands, you knew. And panicked. You tried not to let on that you were about to check out, but this one came hard and fast.

You are standing on the edge of a an isolated forest, the sunlight filtering through the forest canopy. The smell of wood smoke wafts from a fire somewhere nearby. The floor of the forest is covered with wild berries, ferns and slippery, spongy moss. Just past the edge of the woods is a pond. Mountain laurel and hemlock stand out like confetti on the muddy banks and tangled vines hang from the trees tickling the water's surface. It is silent except for the faint, rhythmic recitation of some kind of chanting. You are not alone. A gust of wind causes the vines to sway and brings the distinct sense that something is about to happen...

Thud...Thud....Thud... You opened your eyes and turned your head to see Mason sitting in a lawn chair kicking his feet against the metal base. A cold washcloth was spread across your forehead. Thud...Thud...Thud..."Why are you so weird? Why can't you just be normal like the rest of us? You made Mommy cry," Mason shouted.

"Mason, that's enough. Karen, she's up," David said urgently.

Karen and David helped you sit up. You looked around the yard; all of your guests were gone, your whale cake was still intact, and the candles blown out.

"You all right, sweetie? You gave us a little scare," Karen said as she wiped your face with the washcloth.

"I bet she just had too much sun. Or maybe too much sugar." David ruffled your hair and began clearing the party favors and used plates from the table. But underneath his casual dismissal was a note of concern. You were worried too. Was the shimmering back? Why now? Why you?

You didn't have to wait long to find out. The shimmers came more than ever, and you couldn't always hide them. You knew before anyone else that Mason had 3 cavities. And that the guinea pig in the science classroom was going to have babies. And you didn't want to tell her, but the owner of the craft store where Karen buys her favorite ribbon was going to break her wrist when she trips over a box in the store room. A few months later you overheard Karen and David talking late one night. They hadn't heard you come into the kitchen for a glass of milk. It was technically already lights out. They were sitting in the dining room, and Karen was crying.

"You know I love her, and I've always wanted a daughter. But this just isn't working out, David. Those episodes she has, it's like she goes into her own little world. I mean I knew she had some behavior issues before she came to us, but I thought it was just acting out or being bounced around as a foster kid. I thought once we gave her a loving home and some stability, she wouldn't act like that anymore." Karen stopped to blow her nose loudly into a tattered Kleenex.

"Maybe we'll have to get her some counseling or…I don't know…work with her for a while," David said, trying to comfort Karen.

"We can't afford that. Plus, what if this is the sign of something more serious? It could just get worse. I don't want Mason growing up around someone like that," Karen said through more tears.

"We'll figure something out," David said quietly. You knew what this meant. They were going to send you back. Back to a seedy, smelly bunk bed and two drawers at some drab girls home, probably in a different city. At fourteen, with a file like yours, you had about as much chance of getting adopted, or even fostered, as that kid in Texas who just stabbed his family to death with a screwdriver in the middle of the night.

No, you would figure something out. You had to. Fast. Where could you go where you could live safely on your own, go to school, and not stick out because you don't have any parents hovering over you? It seemed like a miracle when Emily mentioned Susan Short the next day.

"She's two years ahead of us. You know. The only child of the owners of the Short Shoe Factory?" Emily said.

The Short Shoe Factory was the largest business in Hatterly. And the Shorts were the richest family in town.

"What about her?" you asked.

"She went off to boarding school in 10th grade and fell in love with some guy from California. Now she never comes home on school breaks and her parents are thinking of moving to San Diego," Emily answered.

"Boarding school?" you asked. Suddenly you realized it was your answer.

"Yeah, school where you go and sleep over in dorms. Before college. They're supposed to be really hard," Emily added.

Boarding school! It was brilliant! It took care of all of your needs. No one had their parents around. Everyone would be in the same boat as you. Kind of. They would probably let you stay over during school vacations. Somebody would stay behind for breaks.

"Emily, that's it! That's my answer. Boarding school!" you cried out, grasping her shoulder.

Emily squinted at first and looked perplexed. "How would you get in? How would you even figure out where to go?" she asked.

"We'll Google it!" was your retort. Which is exactly what the two of you did that afternoon on Emily's computer. You found an article online entitled, "Tomorrow's Leaders: The Top Ten Boarding Schools in the Country."

"You have awesome grades, and you're in a ton of clubs," Emily pointed out. "You could probably get in to one of these places."

Karen and David couldn't find out about this until you knew for sure if you got in. What if they tried to stop you?

"How do I keep it secret?" you wondered.

"You can use my address. I'm the first one home, and I always check the mail. No one will know but us," Emily announced.

Soon Emily's mailbox began filling up with big white packets, thick questionnaires, writing sample requests, and glossy foldouts of sprawling campuses and grinning, rosy-cheeked students.

"Anywhere but here," was your mantra.

A nice woman in the admissions office at one of the schools explained to you how the entrance exam worked. The good news was that all of the accredited boarding schools used one standardized exam, the SSAT, and there was a test site downtown where you could go and sit for it. The bad news was the test site was downtown and you had to go and sit for it. This meant lying to Karen, something you'd done on occasion but were not very good at.

"Karen, I need to go down to the library tomorrow to research this new history project," you said coolly as Karen finished sewing Mason's Spring Fling costume at the kitchen table.

"Ok, no problem." Karen chirped, not even looking up from her needle and thread.

So that part was easy, but the rest was harder than you thought. While your nose was supposed to be buried in a book, you were catching a stinky bus filled with cranky riders, taking a monster exam that made your brain ache, catching a stinkier bus back, and sprinting to the library steps by five to meet Karen. Somehow, you managed to pull it off.

Then the waiting game began. Most acceptances were sent out the week of March 1st. You and Emily ran to her mailbox each day starting that day.

"Just in case," Emily said. "We don't want to miss one."

On the 3rd, your first answer arrived. The envelope was pretty thin. You sliced it open neatly and began to read. Emily leaned over your shoulder and read along...

"We regret to inform you that this year due to a record number of outstanding applications...." Her voice trailed off.

"It's a no," you said, trying to hide the disappointment in your voice, as you finished reading. Something about more qualified applicants than openings, they encourage you to re-apply the following year, your application was very promising, etc. etc.

"Well that sucks," Emily said. "If they turned you down, it's because that place wasn't right for you." She knit her brow, then got one of her good "Emily" looks.

"I know. We'll burn it," she stated flatly. "Gets rid of the negative energy. Or at least that's what my mom says. Follow me."

Emily's mom is a yoga teacher and knows about these things. She's always talking about energy and vibrations. You once thought about asking her about your shimmers, but you remembered your vow and decided against it.

"Emily, you know you aren't allowed," you warned. Last year Emily got in trouble for starting fires at school during recess. She was burning up her exams marked lower than a B-. Ever since, she has had to fight a pyromaniac rap.

"This is different," she announced airily. She led you to the backyard and lit the letter and envelope with a match.

She did seem to get a gleam in her eye while the paper burned. Actually, over the next week, she got the gleam five more times when she burned five more rejections.

"We're running out of schools," you said feeling disheartened. "Do you think they can tell I'm a foster kid?"

This is your big fear. That foster kids are on some kind of a "Do Not Touch" list that gets passed around schools. Look out, troubled child coming through!

"Of course they can't," Emily answered. "We didn't mention it anywhere. We made sure. Besides, they can't discriminate against you just because you don't have parents. There's gotta be a law against that or something."

"What about the teacher references? We didn't see those," you replied.

"Sure we did," Emily retorted. "I steamed them open. They were good. Ms. Keiffer thinks you're perfect."

Add mail tampering to the list of Emily's foibles.

"Emily!"

She shrugged happily and stuck her tongue out.

For two days nothing arrived. But on March 11th, a gloomy, rainy Tuesday, a huge cream-colored envelope from Trumbull Woodhouse landed on her doorstep. You sat with Emily on her daybed and stared at it.

"I'm afraid," you said. "What if it's another rejection?"

"Just open it! It's big, not like the others. I think that means you got in!" she sang, clapping her hands rapidly like little butterfly wings.

You ripped the envelope open. The paper was so thick it could be fabric. Expensive fabric.

That's when you saw the words you will never forget, "Congratulations, the Admissions Committee of Trumbull Woodhouse has chosen you for a place in the class of …."

You felt a lump in your throat, and your eyes started to sting as hot tears pooled and fell.

"You got in! Oh my god, you got in!" Emily leapt up and ran around her room, laughing and clapping.

You dragged the back of your hand across your eyes to blot your tears and looked up at her. She grabbed your hands and led you around the room in a ring-around-the-rosy style skip fest worthy of Riverdance.

"And it's the best girls' school in the whole country!"

You and Emily celebrated some more the next few days by dancing, singing, cookie baking, and sage burning (of course!). The ceremonies felt good in the moment, but you couldn't ignore this little panicky, not-so-rosy feeling that kept fluttering in your stomach. Tuition at Trumbull Woodhouse was over $48,000 a year. Before books, travel, and uniforms. Now that you were accepted, you had to start worrying about the money part. Your acceptance letter had said that your financial aid package would be forthcoming in approximately ten days. When it arrived, you were nearly as nervous as you were before your acceptance.

"Why did it come to your house?" Emily asked as the two of you closed the mailbox at the end of the driveway. "We never listed your real address. Did you tell Karen and David?"

"No, we agreed I would wait until I had the whole package, remember? I haven't said a thing," you replied.

"That's so weird," Emily replied, stumped by the mail mix up.

You got a tiny shiver up your spine. It *was* strange, you thought.

Moments later you forgot any suspicions when you read the envelope's contents. In one instant, with one sentence, your future goes from terrible to fabulous.

"We are pleased to inform you that a benefactor who wishes to remain anonymous has stepped forward to pay your entire tuition to Trumbull Woodhouse. Provided you maintain a B average or higher, this support will continue for all four years of your time with us."

WHAT?! This was unbelievable! Too good to be true!

"I feel like I could burn my whole house down!" Emily exclaimed, jumping up and down.

Now Karen, David, and Mason stand on one side of the security gate at the Greenville-Spartanburg International airport, and you stand on the other waving good-bye. The airport is only two hours from Hatterly, but you had to stop twice on the way, once for Mason to go to the bathroom and once to get him ice cream. Big surprise. Because of the stops, there was only time for quick hugs. Which is probably better anyway. The closer you got to leaving, the less Karen mentioned coming back for Christmas. The message was clear: you were out of the Donovans' lives for good.

Karen and David wave enthusiastically back as you walk through security, but Mason just stands there in shock. He's not even eating his dip cone from Dairy Queen. That's because on your way to your flight, you left him with some food for thought.

"Scientists just discovered that eating ice cream every day makes your privates fall off. I read it in a magazine, so it has to be true," you whispered in his ear, giving him a little squeeze.

Ok, it was a little mean, but the brat had it coming…

You look at your boarding pass.

""Here you go," the flight attendant says as she points you to your seat. It's a short trip to the third row. "Can I hang your jacket?"

First class? You?

"It's your lucky day because we're serving ice cream to first class after our lunch service," the attendant adds with a wink. You can't believe it. The ticket the school sent was actually first class. You've flown three times in your entire life and always in the cheap seats.

What next, ruby slippers?

You twist in your seat to check out the rest of the plane. A woman a few rows behind in coach you looks up from her magazine and meets your gaze. She smiles over her glasses and you smile back. She looks normal enough, late forties, light grey blouse, curly dark hair, but there's something intense about her stare. It feels like she can see straight through your skin and bones and into your head to read your thoughts. She gives you a little nod and returns to her magazine. You turn back around in your seat. That was a little creepy. Or was it? You don't trust your perceptions lately. All of your senses have felt a little off since you got permission of the state to leave the Donovans (with their rapid blessing) and go to Trumbull Woodhouse.

You pull your book from your backpack, but it's hard to concentrate. You glance up and notice a boy step into the cabin of the plane and pause in the line of passengers filing down the isle. His shaggy mop of brown hair falls haphazardly over his eyes. Despite the late summer heat, he's wearing a striped blazer, like the one Emily's brother has from Urban Outfitters, a local band t-shirt, scores of colorful plastic club bracelets, tight jeans and black

Converse. You don't really think he's cute, but he could be –

Thwack!

He trips and stumbles face first into your lap.

"Oh geez, s-s-sorry," he stammers. Up this close you notice his big green eyes. "I don't even know what made me trip. Are you okay?"

"I'll survive. I think my pinky got crushed," you reply. You try to sound casual, but your finger really does hurt. You take a look. "The nail is still there."

"Ah, yeah. Okay. I'm gonna go find my seat now that I've…tested out yours," he says, standing awkwardly. He smells fresh, like soap and leaves. "Maybe I'll get lucky and take out a few old ladies or someone in a wheelchair," he adds dryly.

"Fifty bonus points for babies," you call over your shoulder.

He laughs and gives you two thumbs up. This reminds you of Emily. She always uses the thumbs up sign, only she meant it sarcastically, as if to say 'yeah right.' That was the hardest part about leaving, saying good-bye to Emily.

She was a mess when you went to her house to hang out one last time the night before last. Her mom made you guys vegan burritos and wild rice, and you had a carpet picnic in Emily's room. (One thing you won't miss about Hatterly: dinner at Emily's.) Emily was crying so hard she choked on a chunk of tofu. You were sad too, but you've been through this many times before. Each time you've switched foster homes or changed schools, you've had to say good-bye to friends, family, teachers, even pets. It's a process that's filled with lots of tears, promises to write, and extra long hugs. The only thing that makes it easier is to not get too attached in the first place.

After takeoff, you pull out the large accordion folder Karen got you to organize the bajillions of papers Trumbull Woodhouse has been sending you all summer. You find the questionnaire you were supposed to have filled out by the time you arrived but have been putting off for weeks. Likes, dislikes, hobbies, fears, dreams...yadda, yadda, yadda. You hate filling out things like this. Just because someone knows you love breakfast for dinner or singing in the bathtub or that feeling you get when you take your feet off the pedals and coast down the hill, or that you hate cauliflower and water getting stuck in your ears doesn't mean they know you. You are greater than the sum of your parts, you want to write. But you begin to fill it out anyway. Just as you get to question 11, you feel a shimmer coming.

There's a red van driving down a highway, weaving gently. It drifts a little into the next lane and then swerves back sharply, as if the driver fell asleep and then woke up and yanked the wheel in terror. But it weaves again. You get this bad feeling that the van is going to crash.

Then just as quickly as the shimmer started, it stops. Thanks a lot, brain, you think to yourself. At least you didn't shimmer a plane crashing, right?

When you return from splashing water on your face in the bathroom, the flight attendant has left a bowl of ice cream on your tray. You sit down and stare at the little mountains covered in hot fudge. You're not really lactose intolerant. That's just one of the excuses you've used over the years, ever since that fateful day in the park with that couple. But now your fate has changed. You changed it. You planned your work, worked your plan, and it actually worked! You have a chance to start a new life, in a new place, with new friends, under new rules, and as a whole new you. Whoever you want to be. So why not be someone who eats ice cream? You plunge your spoon deep into the dish of sweet, gooey, ice cream and take your first wonderful, melt-in-your-mouth bite.

If you had to come up with a name for this flavor, you'd call it Destiny.

"Oh my gosh, you're so smart. Only bring the essentials and FedEx everything else, right?" a girl with long blonde hair and ginormous movie star sunglasses says to you as she puts on another coat of soft pink lip gloss. Her glassy lips move fast and her hands never stop moving through her hair.

You look down at your two suitcases. The truth is, the contents of these two suitcases make-up your entire life and all of your personal possessions. You have some clothes, four pairs of shoes, toiletries, your journal, an iPod Nano David and Karen gave you for your birthday, don't forget your fabulous new underwear, and that's about it, folks.

She, on the other hand, is surrounded by mounds of matching canvas bags and hard luggage pieces with the letters LV plastered all over them. This time last year you would've assumed these were her initials and maybe tried to guess her name out loud, but David surprised Karen with a Louis Vuitton drawstring tote bag for Christmas, so now you're in the know. Thank God. That would've been so embarrassing. The flutter of relief, however, is quickly tugged down by a queasy feeling in the pit of your stomach. There have got to be a million more possible missteps ahead of you, and Karen's Christmas list was only so long. This school, these people, this whole experience is a virtual mine field of humiliation. You decide to stick to the golden rule and keep quiet.

"You'd think I would've learned," the blonde girl continues. "It's not like I'm a Third Former, anymore. My mom had to pay like a bazillion dollars so the airline would let me check all this stuff. She was so pissed..."

The shellacked girl trails off as the driver begins loading her bags into the back of the school van sent to shuttle you and the other arriving girls from the Boston airport to Harrowgate, the town where Trumbull Woodhouse is located.

"Thanks George! How was your summer?" she chirps.

"Fine, thanks, Miss Armstrong," he grunts, as he heaves one of her trunks onto his back. You soon realize that George grunts a lot. And he has freakish upper body strength for a man his age.

"Hailey?! Hi-yeeeee! You look so cuuuuute!" another blonde in similar glasses coos as she runs up and throws her arms around the lip-glossed girl.

The airport doors slide open and two more girls in wispy, flowing summer dresses anchored by rows of delicate gold chain necklaces, charm bracelets, and, yes, even bigger sunglasses spill out. Their flip-flops clap loudly against their feet and their jewelry jingles as they jog up to greet their friends. You all pile into a shiny black passenger van, with the school's name painted discreetly in white.

You notice automatically that it is nothing like the one from your shimmer. Not that you wanted it to be, of course. But once you've had a shimmer, you learn to watch for what it contained. Occasionally you have a random shimmer that doesn't seem to have anything to do with your life and never gets played out in reality. Like the strange forest scene at your Hawaiian-themed birthday a year ago or the woman writing unknown text in glimmering ink when you shimmered at the ice cream shop. But mostly things show up. For the millionth time, you silently wish you understood how this stupid shimmering worked.

The girls chatter straight through the first hour of the drive, through downtown Boston and onto 495. You gather that Hailey is going into her second year at "Trumby," as she refers to it, and Brooke just flew in from her parents' summer home in the Hamptons to begin her third year. Hailey hails from Ohio. You shake your head as you recall the way Hailey spoke at the airport, like she was so far from her days as a freshman, or Third Form as they call it here. Mary Kate and Jasmine are Fifth Formers from Los Angeles. Somehow, Mary Kate and Hailey's older brother dated briefly two summers ago but she insists she's "so over him," which everyone so doesn't believe. Brooke's parents have recently reconciled after a long separation, and Jasmine tried pot for her first time while visiting the set of a music video her father was producing.

It's like reading *US* Magazine, only with normal people's lives substituted for celebrities. All of these girls are so comfortable with one another, you think; they talk alike, dress alike, and even wear the same sunglasses. They all seem to belong. They also have one other thing in common: none of them seem to notice you. This is actually better, you decide. You haven't quite figured out how you're going to spin your past or what details of your life you want to reveal. The less people know about you for now, the better.

"Who are you?" Jasmine finally shouts over the drone of gossip and chatter from the other girls.

Their shared brain must have given the signal to turn around, because the three other girls simultaneously shift around in their seats to look at you.

"Wait…wait…Don't tell me. I should know this. Lemme think for a second," she barks before you can even say a word. "You're definitely a Third Former. You're not the equestrian rider with the big boobs, no offense. You're not the flute player from New Jersey. Are you the girl from D.C. who's dad is that big lobbyist who was caught in a motel with a hooker a couple years ago?"

"No, that's Krissy Christler, remember?" Mary Kate chimes in. "I can't wait to see her."

"Oh yeah. Well, I know you're not the swimmer from Maine, I remember she had red hair…" Jasmine gazes up towards the ceiling, twirling her hair back and forth around her finger as she thinks.

"I know, you're the mystery girl from South Carolina, right?" Jasmine interrupts. She sits up straight. "You never posted a photo, or anything for that matter. There's just a little silhouette outline where your face should be. Nice touch, really."

"What? Post a photo of…myself? Where?" you ask, absolutely gobsmacked by the fact that they know who you are, or at least where you're from.

"The Field," Hailey says casually applying another coat to her lips.

You stare blankly at her. She stops mid-swipe, her bottom jaw dropping open.

"Trumby's version of Facebook? The way we keep up with each other over the summer and get all the gossip before we get back to school? Don't tell me you didn't know about it!" she exclaims in amazement.

You shake your head no.

"Oh, how sad," Brooke cries.

The other girls nod in agreement. You feel the familiar sting of pity as it pierces your pride. And the tug of that feeling in your stomach as you realize a beehive of social interaction has been buzzing and swarming all summer in the airwaves just above your head, and you've been completely left out. Girls were swapping pictures, spreading rumors, sharing inside jokes, funny stories, and favorite things, while friendships formed and bonds crystallized like thick honey.

"Everyone knows everything about everyone at the Crackhouse," Mary Kate explains, using her own nickname for the school. "Think about it. There's only like eighty girls in each class. We go to school together, live together, eat together, play together. That's just the way it is. You'll get used to it."

"At least people know who you are," Brooke says trying to comfort you. "Trust us, there's nothing worse than going faceless all four years. You wanna be known for something. That's very important at our school. Otherwise, you may as well go to public school."

The other girls recoil in disgust at the thought.

Once you're on highway, the inside of the van becomes quiet. Two of the girls have dozed off, heads resting on the windows. Hailey is painting her nails, and Jasmine is listening to her iPod. You watch the lush green landscape of Massachusetts speed past and start to drift off yourself when you catch a flash of red out of the corner of your eye. You sit up straight and crane your neck to see the road ahead. George glances at you curiously in the rearview mirror.

You wait for it, scanning the road with anxious dread. Your heart beats faster. Your breath quickens. It's the van you saw in your shimmer on the plane. You've had shimmers that have played out in real life, but never this soon and never about something so big. So many moments pass that you start to think you imagined the red streak. But then a rusty red van just like the one in your shimmer pulls into the lane ahead of you.

Before you can think, you hear someone call out, "George, can we get off? NOW! TAKE THIS EXIT!"

You suddenly realize it's you who's shouting. So much for keeping your mouth shut. But you couldn't help it. The voice rose up and out of you like you were possessed. Hailey turns around and shoots you a critical look. The other girls stir from the commotion.

"What's going on?" Mary Kate asks, still half asleep.

George gives you a glance in the rearview and deftly shifts into the middle lane, and then toward the exit. He must assume you're sick or something. When you reach the off ramp, he lets up on the accelerator and you glide down the hill, away from the red menace. Right away your stomach begins to unclench. As you reach the stop sign at the end of the exit, there is a massive BOOM! followed by the sick crunch of metal. You look up just as the red van flips and tumbles on the highway fifty yards ahead, exploding in a ball of flame.

"Whoa. Did you see that?!" Brooke shouts. "Look!"

You watch as the highway traffic swerves to avoid the fireball. The air is filled with the scream of squealing brakes as an entire interstate of cars grinds to a halt. George pulls across the street into a parking lot for commuters. The girls surge out of the van and run to the edge, straining to see the calamity. The sound of more metal smashing on metal tells you there are secondary accidents. A cloud of thick black smoke streams into the air from the van which is burning to a crisp.

George wipes his brow nervously and looks at you. "How did you know there was going to be an accident?" he asks simply. Everyone stares at you.

"I... I didn't," you stammer. "I...I just had to go to the bathroom. Really badly," you add, feeling your cheeks turn red. "Sorry."

Everyone looks back to the wreckage, accepting your explanation. Everyone but George, who holds his stare a beat longer. It's not like you are about to explain your shimmers to total strangers. Much less schoolmates you will be spending the next four years with.

"Come on then, " George says as the sound of distant sirens grows louder. "We need to find a restroom, and get on our way."

"I have to use one too," Jasmine says.

You climb back in the van. Everyone talks about the accident. Or at least everyone except you. You stop at a nearby gas station just as a fire truck speeds past and heads onto the exit ramp you just descended.

Once inside the restroom, you splash your face with cold water and look at your fractured reflection in the cracked mirror. You look normal on the outside. Inside you feel like a tornado has been unleashed in your head. Of course you're glad you saved yourself and the others from harm, but you can't believe you saw that crash so perfectly! What does it mean? Are you going to continue to be bombarded with images of disasters right before they happen? And run around alerting everyone like the Chicken Little of Trumbull Woodhouse? You scowl at yourself in the mirror as a warning to your broken brain.

There is a knock on the restroom door. "We're getting slushies. Do you want one?" Jasmine's muffled voice calls through the door.

You shake off your shimmer and flash a big smile in the mirror. *There, that's more like it.* You open the door.

"No thanks," you reply, trying to sound upbeat.

"Thank God you had to pee or we may have been on the road when that accident happened," she says as she squeezes by. "Ew, it's so gross in here. I'm definitely hovering," you hear her say as she closes the bathroom door.

Thank God they believed your story about needing the bathroom.

George stays off the highway for the rest of your trip, sticking to back roads. About an hour later you reach Harrowgate. You are so preoccupied and nervous, you don't notice much about the town as you pass through. You are still turning over the events with the red van in your head. George turns on to a rolling paved road where traffic thins out. You pass several enormous, rambling houses set back from the street. Some are so big they could pass for small hotels. You read somewhere that Harrowgate was a wealthy farming community founded in the 18th century. It looks like the money just kept piling up. A low stone wall appears on your right, and the fields beyond it are perfectly manicured and neat, not a blade of grass out of place.

"Here we are," George announces, slowing to turn onto school grounds.

The van slips underneath an ornate, iron-scrolled entrance gate framed by huge trees on both sides. Just past the arch, you feel an overwhelming rush of tingling and heat, like a current of electricity is coursing through your veins while the sound of rushing water fills your head. What the heck is this? you think. Then as suddenly as it starts, the tingling and rushing stops. You look around. Jasmine looks a little perplexed. But no one else has noticed a thing.

You look ahead to the largest sprawl of lawn you have ever seen. It's surrounded by all the buildings you recognize from the catalog and website. Three mountains tower in the distance.

Toto, I have a feeling we're not in Kansas anymore.

George pulls the van into a procession of cars that snakes through the middle of campus. Cars, vans, and limos are pouring in and pulling up from every direction as the girls of Trumbull Woodhouse return to their home away from home for another year. You watch smartly dressed parents shake hands and show off their daughters all across the lawns and in front of the residential halls. There are twenty-one dorms in all, scattered like popcorn over the four hundred acres of main campus. You notice that their style and architecture hint at the era in which each building was added on. And with names like Bloomer, Winfrey, Curie, Cassatt, and Alcott, every dorm honors an influential woman in history.

One by one, George pulls up to a dorm, unpacks some luggage and a van mate hops out. The last girl to get dropped off besides you is Hailey. Her dorm, Grimke Hall, reminds you of old gothic churches, with puffy stone walls, pointy spires, and menacing gargoyles watching you from every corner. She's been very chatty, volunteering Trumby history factoids after a fresh coat of lip varnish. But when George pulls the van to a halt and jumps out, she turns to you, lowers her designer goggles to the tip of her nose, and stares you down with steely gray eyes flecked by bits of amber.

"Tell me something, South Carolina," she says quietly. "You knew that red van was going to crash, didn't you? Before it happened." She chews on her gum, her jaw snapping open and shut like a shiny-lipped crocodile, waiting for your answer. Her confrontational approach takes you by surprise. But you try to stay calm. Don't let your voice shoot up six octaves to a high-pitched squeak like it wants to, you think, taking a deep breath.

"That would be a cool trick, " you fib, "being able to see the future. But like I said, I just had to go to the bathroom. Really, really badly," you add firmly. You try to shrug casually. George pulls open the sliding van door.

"All right, Miss Armstrong," he says.

Hailey's eyes don't move for a moment. They stay locked on yours. As much as you want to look down, you know better.

"Right, how could you?" she says casually. The corners of her mouth flick up into a smile and her glasses slide back into place. "See you around. Good luck with everything." She bounces out of the van and slams the door. You sit back against the warm leather seat. What on earth made her suspect you? Was it the way you had called out to George? There's no way Hailey could know about your shimmers. You just hope your explanation made sense and that your nerves didn't show. Your pulse throbs. You take some more deep breaths. You feel relief when George gets back behind the wheel and throws the van into gear.

"Next up, Rose House," he announces, pointing the van and

you, in the direction of your new home.

Two minutes later you pull up to a three story, weathered brick building with white trim. Terracotta flower boxes line each window, and a blooming rose vine creeps up the sides to the third floor.

"Don't worry," you tell George. "I've got it," you say as you grab your two measly suitcases. You've carried your own bags from home to home since you were five. Trumbull Woodhouse won't be changing that.

"Thanks for the ride," you say cheerily.

"I should be thanking you, young lady," is all he says. He gives you a curt nod – George is not overly active in the smile department – and gets back behind the wheel. The parking area outside Rose House is quiet. Nobody else is unloading right now. A lull, you think. Good timing.

Your arrival is announced by the rhythmic crunch of your sneakers on the pebbled walkway. Just inside the door, there is a knobby legged, antique table covered with envelopes. Each one has a name printed on the front flap, yours being one of them. A tray of finger sandwiches and cookies sits alongside a big pitcher of pink lemonade.

A door is open to the right of the table. A 35-ish man in khakis and a slender woman in a yellow cotton dress and ballet flats are seated in their living room, drinking cups of tea. He's stately; she looks like a chic version of Betty Crocker. Side by side, they look like morning TV talk show hosts.

"Hello! Welcome!" the man says, rising.

"You must be one of our new residents," the woman says pleasantly as she gets up to greet you.

"We're Gordon and Lily Mitchell. Your dorm parents," she explains. You set down your suitcases to shake their hands and introduce yourself. They both nod knowingly when you tell them your name. "It's great to finally meet you. You were the only one we couldn't read about on The Field this summer," Lily Mitchell says.

You grimace. "I know. I never got my email invitation I guess. I heard about it in the van from the airport. So I'm the only one who didn't join in the fun. I wish I had known about it."

"Oh, don't feel bad. Plenty of time to get to know everyone. That's the beauty of boarding school," Gordon assures you. "How was the flight from South Carolina? Not too bumpy, I hope."

Thanks to The Field mishap, your place of origin is the only fact everyone seems to know about you. But now that you've seen inside the Emerald City, you're sure they've done their homework on every student.

"My flight was great," you reply, praying they don't ask you about the drive from the airport.

"Well, good. You're in Suite 2B, up on the second floor. And I believe you are the first to arrive?" Lily looks over at her husband for confirmation.

"Yes she is. Follow me." Gordon Mitchell grabs your suitcases and bounds up the stairs. You follow closely behind. A car pulls up into the crescent moon drive in front of Rose House, so Lily heads out to greet the latest arrivals.

"Here we are," Gordon announces. There are three doors at the top of the landing, one to each side and one straight ahead.

"That door leads to the second floor baths and showers," he says, nodding in the direction of the door in the middle. "Rose House has three suites to a floor, and four girls to each suite." He opens the lacquered black door on the left. It leads into a common living room with a thick, patterned rug covering the honey-colored wood floors.

You smell a fresh coat of paint. The white trim glistens, not a spec of dust yet. The room contains a dark tan couch, two red paisley chairs, and two side tables with blue and white Chinese lamps. It looks more like a luxury hotel than the dorm rooms you've seen on TV. Four small single bedrooms lead off the common room.

You follow Gordon to the farther one on the right. The name of each of your suitemates is printed on a card taped to the door of her assigned room. You say the others' names in your head as you pass by and peek in their rooms: Hayden Murdoch, Willa Nash, and Casey Mulligan. You notice that each room contains a twin bed, a petite desk and chair, two small, small closets, and a dresser.

"Here you are. Home sweet home," Gordon says with a wink as he opens the door to your room. You can't believe your eyes.

"This... is my room?" you ask in amazement. You take three steps inside and turn slowly, taking it all in. The room is beautiful and by far the best one in the suite. It has the same furniture as the others, but it's on a corner, so it is a little bigger and doesn't feel as cluttered. You have two windows, where the other girls only have one, and you have your very own...wait for it... marble fireplace! You've seen them in movies and the decorating magazines Karen reads, but never in real life. You rush over to the windows. You can see the tops of peoples' head milling around below and three majestic mountains in the distance.

"Fireplace doesn't work, unfortunately," Gordon says, setting your bags on the floor. "But it's nice to have anyway."

You nod. You are speechless.

"I should get back downstairs," Gordon says. "And I am sure you are eager to unpack. Your roommates will be here soon, so enjoy the quiet while you have it," Gordon warns. "We're right downstairs if you need anything at all. There's a quick meeting just before dinner at 5:45 to explain sign-in and sign-out. See you then. And I think someone will drop by to take you on a campus tour here shortly. So be aware."

"Thanks," you say.

Gordon pulls the door behind him, leaving it open a crack. You take his advice and sit on your bed, taking a few deep breathes. This is the perfect time to perform a little ritual you like to do each time you land in a new room at a new home. With your eyes closed, you picture the room and every tiny detail you can remember about it. You imagine yourself living in here each day, reading, sleeping, studying, writing in your journal, talking to friends, getting dressed.

You say out loud, "This is my room now. This is where I live. This is my home. I am going to have a fabulous life here."

"Heloooo? Knock-knock," says a girl with a long, horsey face and flat dirty-blonde hair, as she opens your door and interrupts your mantra. She wears all-black workout gear and a T-shirt that says "In Trumbull We Trust," and carries a field hockey stick.

"Hi! I'm Regan Jenner. I'm a Sixth Former and your upperclass Orienteer." Regan reaches forward to shake your hand. She has a grip like a Russian lady wrestler.

"Hi," you say. You can't tell why but you immediately feel on guard. Maybe because she's acting so overly friendly and familiar, but in a forced way. Or maybe it's the way her eyes flicker as she gives you the once over.

"Gordon mentioned someone would be around," you add.

"Right. I'm your personal tour guide today. Don't worry, everybody gets one. And any time you have a question about how things work here at TW, I'm here with answers. I live right over there," she adds, pointing to another dorm that you can just make out through the trees.

You nod. You get a small shiver up your spine and decide to grab a sweater.

"Ready to begin the best year four years of your life? Follow me," she continues. You can't tell if she's being serious, or trying to be sarcastic.

Outside, you and Regan wave to Gordon and Lily who are greeting a new arrival in the parking lot. Regan whips out her campus map, the same one you received in your admissions packet, but hers looks a wee bit different. It's been blown up, laminated, and tricked out with puff paint, glitter, and comments floating in crinkly clouds.

"I'm sure you took the guided tour when you came to visit, right?" she asks, already assuming the answer is yes. She catches herself when you stare back at her blankly.

"You mean you didn't come for an overnight during host week? Not even a day visit?" she asks incredulously.

"Uh, no. I'm from South Carolina. My application was... um...a bit last minute. But I went through the photo gallery on the website about a hundred times," you say, your voice going up an octave on the last word so it sounds more like a question than an answer.

"Wow. My parents and I checked out eleven different schools before I chose this one." She shakes her head in disbelief. "I can't imagine choosing a school without seeing it first."

You just shrug and smile.

"Anyhow," she continues, "we are standing here." She points to a spot in the center of the map. "This hot pink area where I drew all the stars is considered main campus." Her hand traces a large circle rimmed in black. "It's about four hundred acres total, but a lot of that is taken up by the playing fields, the lake, and the cross-country running trails that extend up and into the woods. It's basically everything you see around us and where you'll be spending your day-to-day life. All those little glittery squares on the map are the buildings where you'll go to class, eat, study, hang out, workout, go to chapel, etc. I know it looks like a big area, but I'll show you everything you need to know today to survive. And it gets familiar fast. Ready?"

You nod vigorously, trying to keep up as she trots along.

As you crest the hill near the cluster of quaint cottages housing the faculty offices, you reach the Great Lawn. It must be ten acres. The expanse is mostly flat, but on the far side there are marble steps cut into a gentle incline and a mosaic of flower beds. Picnic tables, chaise lounges, and umbrella'd settees dot the grassy cul de sac.

"It's the gathering place for the 'Who's Who,' the 'Who's That?' and the 'Who Cares' of the student body," Regan explains as you walk across the gigantic plush lawn. "Those fields over there in the distance are the Upper Fields, and those way down there are the Lower Fields. Betcha can't guess how they got their names?" Regan says. Now she *is* being sarcastic.

You smile and nod at her joke. But inside you're just glad there will be at least two places you can actually remember.

"That group of buildings to the left and right of the rotunda are all the classrooms. The ones on the right are for Humanities, Languages, and Performing Arts. The buildings on the left are your Mathematics, Sciences, and Visual Arts. And that big rotunda in the middle with all the balloons is the student center. That's where we're headed next."

Regan hurries ahead. She is surprisingly fast for having such stubby legs. You have to speed walk just to keep up. Even so, you are a half pace behind.

As you traverse the Great Lawn, something odd catches your eye. Older men in black suits, mirrored sunglasses, and earpieces are lurking around the tables and among the classroom buildings. They stand out like black thumbs among all the greenery. You stare at them for a few moments, your feet slowing, your pumping arms dropping to your sides. They stoop to check under tables and radio inaudible messages into their microphones. What's going on?

"Hey!" Regan shouts, seeing you fall behind. You sprint to catch up and ask her about it.

"What's with the men in black?" you ask.

Her eyes narrow. "Those are the security guards for Chloe LaFleur," she says dryly, rolling her eyes. "She's the daughter of the French Ambassador to the US. It's been all over The Field. You know about The Field, right?"

"Yeah, I learned about it today on my way from the airport."

Regan doesn't seem to think this is strange.

"You should definitely join up. It's a great way to get to know folks," she counsels.

You reach the Student Center and push open the door. You are both met with a blast of cold air and a quiet roar of hubbub and commotion. You follow closely behind Regan as she weaves her way through the human ant farm of activity. Girls and their parents are searching around and taking their place in lines at tables and booths under archways of balloons and streamers.

Regan leads you to a table where you receive a thick white accordion file with the school crest embossed in gold foil on the side. A severe woman whose nametag says "Ms. Moss" checks your name off a master list, giving you a stern once-over through the thick lens of her horn rimmed bi-focals. "You'll do," she says to no one in particular.

You open the folder. It contains your class schedule, the name of your advisor, your laptop voucher, and your mailbox number and key. There is a note attached to the key that says it will cost $10 to replace it. As you flip through the various papers, reading, Regan stops one more time in front of an imposing antique desk. An old embroidered banner hangs just above that says "The Registry" in script so fancy it's hard to decipher.

A robust woman sits poised at the desk. Her hair is tightly coiled in a bun on the crown of her head. She hands you a jewel-encrusted fountain pen with real ink, and pushes a very large leather bound book toward you.

"This is the official registry for the school," she explains in a soft, steady voice. Her knobby finger points to a line where your full name is printed in big bold letters. The book smells like expensive leather and old paper. The month and year is written out at the top of the page in gold, red, blue and black ink, like an illuminated manuscript from the Middle Ages. "Your signature is your word. It represents your sincere commitment to uphold the Trumbull Woodhouse name and strictly abide by all rules of the institution both on and off campus," she explains. You glance at Regan who nods encouragingly.

Well when you put it that way…who could resist?

Regan and Hairdo Lady watch closely as you awkwardly sign your full name, trying to use your best cursive. At that instant, the front door blows open and a gust of wind sweeps through the hall. Papers flutter and women's hands hold down the hemlines of their skirts. Everyone turns to look, but there's nothing and no one there. Just the wind. So they return to their tasks. One of the administrative aides rushes over to close the door and secure it.

Strange, you think, you were just outside moments ago, and there wasn't even a breeze. Where did that come from?

"Congratulations!" Regan says perfunctorily. "You're officially a Trumbull Woodhouse Lampyridae!" She notices your nose crinkle and your quizzical look. "Or firefly, in plain English," she adds. "As in flying bug that glows. It's our school mascot."

She checks her watch. "Okay, we need to get you to your mailbox. It'll be overflowing with snail mail."

Sure enough, when you unlock your mailbox with your ten dollar key, it's stuffed!

"It's like the teachers here have never heard of the internet," Regan laughs out loud. "The coaches too. They love leaving you notes and reminders. Plus schedules, menus, and personal mail from the real world."

You unwedge the cards, notes, and slips of paper from the rectangular opening. The schedule for soccer practice and JV tryouts is on top. Ugh. Underneath is a reminder to come by the Counting House tomorrow to discuss your account – bigger Ugh – a time slot to go pick up your uniform tomorrow, a dauntingly thick School Handbook, and a copy of "The History of Trumbull Woodhouse Campus." Printed on flocked paper with a blue ribbon looped through a hole at the top is an invitation to the Headmistress's Luncheon on Sunday following Convocation. There is one last piece of mail — a pale blue envelope with your name written in black calligraphy on the cover. But before you have a chance to open it, Regan returns from her mailbox.

"Good thing we came by our boxes. My field hockey meeting got moved up. I want to show you the school store and Snack Shack before I have to go. You'll thank me later. C'mon."

When you walk into the Nest, the nickname for the student store, you see why Regan loves it. It's bigger, nicer, and carries more products than the grocery store and department store combined in Hatterly! The Nest has everything from cosmetics and magazines to shoes and school supplies, just about anything you would ever need.

"So here's how it works. It's open from 8 AM to 7 PM. Come in here, grab whatever you need, and just charge it to your school account. It gets deducted from the money your parents deposit," Regan explains simply.

Unfortunately, that's not exactly how it's going to work for you, but you don't want to burst her bubble. Connected to the Nest is the Snack Shack where girls can come in between classes for burgers, candy, milkshakes, and some social time. With little booths, couches, and overstuffed chairs, it feels like someone's living room. Suddenly, a herd of girls roves in and descend upon Regan.

As they ooh and ahh over their summers, you open that envelope with the elaborate calligraphy. It's another invitation. This one from your advisor, Elizabeth Wilmingtom, who wants you to come to her cottage late tomorrow afternoon at 4:30 sharp. She actually wrote the word "sharp". The appointments are racking up but this one stands out because of the handwriting. It's the same looping, curling, rolling letters in rich black ink as on the outside of the envelope. Every word is perfectly aligned and spaced, like the way fairytales are written.

"Whatcha got there?" Regan asks, returning from her friends.

"Oh, my Advisor invited me to her house tomorrow," you reply, focusing all your attention on putting the note back in the envelope without bending the corners.

"Oh! Who'd you get?" Regan sticks her face in front of yours forcing you to give her attention.

"Elizabeth Wilmington."

You see a flash of irritation register on Regan's face. Her eyes squint as her pupils dilate into two black pools. For a split second, she looks almost sinister.

"Are you sure? Willie hasn't been an advisor for quite a while. She's one of the legends around here. I don't think she'd take on an advisee," Regan says trying to hide her suspicion behind a smile.

You carefully pull out the invite and show her the note. "It's also in my paperwork, see?" You flip through the papers in your folder to the page listing the names of your dorm parents, teachers, roommates, and advisor.

"Huh. So it is," Regan says with a firm nod. All traces of her jealousy, annoyance, or whatever that mood was is gone. "Okay, then. I have to go to my meeting, but I'll walk you back to your dorm first."

"I think I'm going to stick around here for a minute and maybe pick up a few things at the store," you tell her. It's a lie, of course. You can't afford to buy anything. But you want to look around a little on your own.

"See ya at supper," she calls as she trots off, crossing off an item on her clipboard. "Good luck with everything."

Is it possible this is one, long dream?

After Regan leaves, you wander around the Student Center for a little while, before departing to cross back over the Great Lawn to Rose House. Fourteen years of life so far have taught you not to expect too much. A clean toothbrush, your own room, a twinkling tree at Christmas, a family to enjoy it with – this is as big as you allow yourself to dream. Reach any higher and the gap between what is and what you want it to be would swallow you whole. That's why that irksome little voice inside your head had to be silenced long ago, the one that whispered to you during the hazy moments just before sleep or the surreal seconds just before awakening.

There's something bigger out there waiting for you.

But what was it? A real mom and dad someplace? A secret inheritance? A missing piece to the puzzle that would make all your loneliness make sense? You would hear the voice, reach for it, and wake up only to be reminded that it wasn't real, just a voice echoing a dream.

You gaze around the campus as you walk. It all seems pretty real. Surprising maybe, but real. Bizarre that you would be here, but real. You turn the corner to Rose House just as four muscle-bound men stagger out of two moving trucks parked on the gravel in front. They look like overburdened pack mules as they lug an antique carved oak desk, a cherrywood four poster bed frame, and several framed canvases. For a minute you wonder what's going on and then you realize. It belongs to students moving in.

"What is this place?" you wonder out loud, and literally pinch yourself one last time to make sure.

When you reach your suite at the top of the stairs, a brown-haired, tom-boyish, surprisingly curvy girl is standing at the window in the common room waving to someone below.

"Hey!" you say, eager to meet your new roommate.

She turns, still waving. "Oh hey!" I'm Casey. Casey Mulligan," she says, her other hand reaching out to shake yours. You cross the room to join her at the window and introduce yourself. She's wearing a t-shirt, jeans, and a baseball cap that says "I ❤ The Planet." She's brainy-looking but very cute with tiny, light brown freckles dotting her little bunny nose and tanned round cheeks.

"Who are you waving to?" you ask curiously.

"Oh, see that black Mercedes in the parking lot down there?" she asks pointing through the window. You nod. "Those are my parents."

You look closer and see a woman with her head down typing furiously on her Blackberry. Casey's dad is backing out but already on his Bluetooth headset. Neither of them are waving back. "They're both doctors," Casey says apologetically.

"Apparently there's no cell phone service on campus, and their answering services are freaking out." Casey watches them go, turning her hands up to the air and shrugging her shoulders. "Back to Bar Harbor they go," she says with a weak smile.

"I'm sorry I didn't get to meet them." It sounds like the right thing to say but you're secretly relieved you didn't have to. You look past Casey's shoulder and see your two suitcases in the hallway.

"Are those *my* suitcases?" you say out loud.

Casey turns and rolls her eyes. She winces as she informs you, "Yeah. I think you got Murdoched."

"I got what?" you ask.

"Murdoched, as in Hayden Murdoch. She's one of our other suite mates," Casey explains, pointing to your room. She leans forward and whispers, "And according to my sources, a real piece of work. Not in the good sense."

The little card on your bedroom door has been switched. It now reads "Hayden Murdoch." You slowly push it open, expecting to face a big, burly, bully, like the one who used to take your pillow from your bed and use it to prop up her feet at one of the girls' homes. But instead, you see a living Barbie Doll sitting on an upholstered footstool in pink, marabou slippers. She's gazing into a bedazzled hand-held mirror fluffing her layered blonde hair. As she admires her bleach-perfect teeth in her reflection, she notices you standing there.

"Yes? Can I help you?" she asks, never taking her eyes off herself.

"Um, I think you made a mistake. This is supposed to be my room," you say with all the good will you can muster.

"Oh! You must be one of the roommates. Were those your bags that were in here? That's so funny, I thought the maid had left them or something. Oh, well. I hope you don't mind, but I need the extra light," she says as she gestures to the room. She has already taken the liberty of hanging bright pink curtains, ornate gold sconces, a gigantic mirror, and an oil painting portrait of herself posing with a small furball of a dog. The once barren bed is covered with a checked pale pink duvet and several patterned throw pillows in different shades of pink.

Mind? Of course you mind. This brat just stole your room. Who does she think she is? you think to yourself, the anger welling up inside you. You can't make a scene, but are you really gonna let Goldilocks sleep in your bed? Luckily, before you have to choose either way, Poppa Bear comes to the rescue.

"Girls? Is it okay if I come in?" Gordon's bass and gravel voice rumbles from the living room. He appears in the doorway. Casey stands just behind him and gives you a wink. She's called in the cavalry. Good roommate and even better friend.

"I was just coming up to change a light bulb next door, and thought I'd check in on you. Hayden, isn't your room across the hall?" he rolls smoothly from one topic to the next.

"It was, but I think there's been some mix up. This room clearly suits me better," she says in a syrupy sweet tone.

"I'm sorry Hayden, there was no mix up. I put the cards up myself. Everyone must live in the rooms they were assigned. School rules," he says gently, trying to bring her around.

"But I need the light, and I have way more stuff than she does," her tone turning to a whine.

"That may be so, but we can't have everyone switching rooms at the last minute; it would be chaos. I'm sure you can understand," he says gently but firmly.

"But..." she begins her plea again.

"Hayden. This is not up for discussion. Lily and I will move the big things while you're at dinner. But in the meantime, take your clothing and luggage to your room." His gentle urging hardens into a firm command. Poppa Bear has spoken. He softens again as he holds up the light bulb. "Now excuse me while I go brighten someone's day."

Hayden stands up in a huff worthy of Hollywood and scowls at you. "You little tattle tale. You think you're so special. Have your stupid room. I'll get even. Just wait and see." She grabs a few items and breezes past you into her room, slamming the door behind her.

Casey runs into her room and motions you to follow. She closes the door behind you, dissolving into giggles.

"That...was...awesome," she says through her laughter. "C'mon, let's go walk around before dinner. I don't want to be cooped up in here with the drama queen."

You and Casey discover a rose garden in full bloom behind one of the dorms and find a bench to sit.

"Who is she?" you ask, still shaking your head.

"I got the scoop from my cousin Jenny. She was in Hayden's class at the same day school in New York," Casey explains. "Hayden is notorious there, and believe me, at a place like Shipman, that's saying something. Jenny said she was the biggest Queen Bee ever to walk the halls of that school."

"Really?" you ask, not surprised.

"Oh yeah, she grew up on the Upper East side, but she thinks she's related to the British royal family. I'm talking total bitch. Her parents are loaded, of course. Her dad runs a hedge fund and her mom is an interior designer. Her parents are big wigs in the New York social scene. Her mom was even on the Committee for the Costume Institute Gala last spring."

You nod as if you know what that means.

"I don't get it. Why do bratty, selfish, mean girls get rewarded with a rich family and a perfect life?" you wonder out loud, a twinge of jealousy flaring up in your chest. Even though you just met Casey, you feel comfortable enough with her to voice this frustration.

"Well, being spoiled usually turns you into a bratty, selfish person. And I seriously doubt her life is as perfect as she acts. In my experience, there's always a dark, dirty underbelly to every life, no matter how shiny and pretty it looks on top."

"Whatever it is, it doesn't seem to stop her from acting like a royal pain in the ass," you say, sighing.

Casey nods in agreement. "I can only imagine what she'll be like when she gets her period," she says. You both start to laugh again.

Casey pauses. "You know, it's good to finally meet you. After you never responded to any of my friend requests on The Field this summer, I didn't know what to expect."

"I never got your requests," you tell her. "Or anybody else's. My email invite to join The Field never arrived. It might have come and might have been, well...I never received it. Things are kind of complicated for me at home."

Casey cocks her head, puzzled.

"You think it was deleted before you got it?" Casey asks, eyes wide.

You shrug. "Maybe accidentally. Or my little brother could've trashed it. I don't have my own computer. I'm here on a total scholarship, all expenses paid. I don't have the money for a place like Trumbull Woodhouse," you tell her.

She nods sympathetically.

It's not the full truth. But it's as much as you feel comfortable saying right now. You're sure you'll tell Casey about being a foster kid one of these days. You can just feel it. But not yet. You're not ready.

"Everyone here is so rich, and smart, and pretty, and well dressed. And I'm...not. I already feel like I don't really belong here."

"No way!" Casey announces confidently. "I've only known you an hour and I'm certain you belong here. Certainly as much as I do. And my certainty overcomes your doubt," she adds with a decisive nod. Her tone is so personal and sincere. She almost convinces you on the spot. And at that moment, as her little chipmunk cheeks puff up into a benevolent smile, you know you and Casey are going to be great friends.

And that little voice inside your head whispers *'I told you so.'*

Casey checks her watch. It's 5:45, time for your dorm meeting about sign-in and sign-out. But it turns out to last all of about two seconds.

"There's a place for your name, the time you leave, where you're going, and then a place to initial when you return," Lily explains, pointing to a clipboard on the front hall table.

While she talks, your new dormmates stream past and seem to already know what to do. They casually add their names to the sign-out sheet, and the word "Dinner" as their destination. You and Casey follow right behind. About twenty minutes later, you're standing in the food line in one of the two industrial kitchens on either end of the Carson Dining Hall. Your room is being returned to its original, undecorated, un-Haydened state by your dorm parents at the same time that mouth-watering filet mignon, piping hot mashed potatoes, and buttered green beans are spooned onto your tray by uniformed staff.

"Don't get used to this," an older looking girl ahead of you in line snipes over her shoulder. "It's back to sloppy joes once the parents are all gone."

There is a separate cold buffet and salad bar that you and Casey plan to visit after you've found a table. You spot a couple of open seats. Just as you sit, you hear Hayden's distinctive high-pitched voice behind you.

"So picture this. It's the day Julienne Dresser's agent wants to meet me for lunch at Bangle in SoHo. The car service is coming at noon, so I figure I have plenty of time to relax, right? Wrong! Ines, the new housekeeper, decides to wash my new Prada cashmere knee-highs in hot water and practically sets them on fire in the dryer. They're ruined. Wouldn't fit a Barbie Doll. Then she forgets the whipped cream in my caramel macchiato, doesn't change Trixie's wee pad, and brings me an omelet with..." The other girls at the table lean forward in suspense. "...yolks! I mean, what is this, the apocalypse?" Hayden croaks in disbelief.

"Somebody's getting fired," her sidekick sings as she finishes painting on her dark purple eyeliner. With a slight flick of her wrist, she creates the perfect cat eye. But try as she might, no amount of dramatic make-up will distract anyone from the bandages on her nose.

"That's Erica Cho," Casey whispers. "Her mom married husband number four last year. He's a renowned plastic surgeon and was one of Chicago's most eligible bachelors. Now she and her mom are a constant 'work in progress,'" Casey informs you, raising her eyebrows.

You glance back at Erica and wince. She has smooth Asian features, wide green eyes, and dark black hair. You wonder why a girl who was so pretty to begin with would want to change anything? A nose job at 14?

The girl next to her with flawless olive skin and sugar spun hair picks at a plate of steak cut into tiny pieces. A colorful Hermes scarf is tied in an intricate knot around her neck. "What is that moronic rule again? We have to stay on campus without leaving for three weeks? Because we're new girls?" She rolls her eyes in disgust.

"Three whole weeks until we can see a boy?" Erica chokes. She reaches for a sip of water. "You cannot be serious."

"As serious as a heart attack," her friend replies, listlessly moving the meat around on her plate.

Casey leans forward again. "Danielle Maldonado," she whispers. "Both she and Erica went to Shipman with Hayden. They are her loyal followers," she adds quietly. "Do you want anything? I'm going to get some salad."

You shake your head no, and continue to gaze surreptitiously at Hayden's table. They dress in a similar style. What do they call it? Oh yeah, rich. Hayden carries a giant flowered bag that you swear you saw in Karen's copy of last month's Vogue. Erica's shiny patent leather hobo hangs like a protected silk cocoon on its own chair. All of their fingers, earlobes, wrists, and necks are draped with delicate gold jewelry. Each outfit is layered, colorful, and obviously expensive, right down to their painted toes in their shiny gold sandals.

Hayden catches you staring and scowls. She whispers something to Danielle and Erica who turn around and shoot withering death glares at you.

"Is anyone sitting here?" someone asks. You whirl around.

"No, please have a seat," you say, turning to face two girls who look like twins but turn out to be first cousins.

Casey comes back with a heaping plate of salad and chats them up. One of the two is the Girls Junior National Archery

Champion. "Nothing else to do in Idaho, except shoot," she explains cheerfully.

"Hey," says the other twin, peering at you more curiously. "Aren't you the girl who saved everybody from that car accident on the airport shuttle? Hailey said you're practically a psychic."

Casey gives you a surprised look.

"Just lucky, I guess," you say, feeling a twinge of embarrassment.

You and Casey finish dinner a few minutes later, say good-night to the Idaho girls, and head back to Rose House. When you get there, your fourth roommate has just arrived on the last shuttle from Logan Airport. Willa Nash is tall, thin, and tan, with a thatch of thick sun bleached hair chopped short and uneven, like she did it herself. She skips the handshake and gives you both a hug in-stead. As she pulls away her black nail-polished fingers reflexively adjust the small gold ring wrapped snugly around the left nostril of her nose. She's not standard issue Trumbull Woodhouse, that's for sure.

"I love your outfit," you say, admiring her funky dress and half boots.

"Oh, thanks. My mom picked up this dress for me in New York. She had a gallery exhibit last spring," she says without an ounce of pretense. She looks to be in the midst of unpacking several large, somewhat strange sculpture/paintings made out of stones and painted clay and rusted cans and bits of wire and string and paper. More miniature paintings and other objects are tucked into flat spots and hidden spaces.

"This stuff is great," Casey says admiringly. "Is it your mom's?" she asks.

"No, no. My mom's work is much more traditional. This is my stuff," Willa tells you, heaving one of them up so it sits on her desk, covering most of it.

"I don't believe in paying for art supplies, if I can help it," she explains. "Why would you when you can find them on any sidewalk, or in any dumpster, park, field, or stream for free?" she asks turning up her palms and rocking back on her heels. "I call it bio-art."

Casey, who turns out to be a devoted environmentalist, instantly becomes an admirer. You are fascinated by the small painted bits that look like the frescoes from Pompeii that you saw in a book once at the Hatterly library.

A few minutes later, while you're still admiring Willa's work, Hayden comes into the suite, handmaidens Erica and Danielle in tow. You look at the clock. 8:30. According to the rules book, Hayden's guests have another half hour before they turn into pumpkins. Already, it feels very different than home. There is this slightly dangerous and exhilarating freedom in the air. Your time is your own. It's 8:30 and there is no parent to report to. You get to do anything you want. Well, anything that doesn't break one of the four crajillion rules in the Handbook.

Hayden is much nicer to Willa when she meets her than she was to you or Casey. She doesn't even glance in your direction despite the fact that both of you are standing six inches away from the object of her attention. And whatever Hayden does, her friends copy exactly so Danielle and Erica stare right past you too. It's so rude it's funny.

"My mom thinks your mom's work is fucking fantastic," Hayden gushes. "She says your mom is one of the hottest artists out there right now. And my mom would know. She's like the hottest interior designer on the East Coast. She's doing Madonna's penthouse next month." Hayden manages to brag, suck up, and name drop all at the same time. She turns to her own personal fan club. "Danielle. Erica. I don't think you get it. There's a three year wait-list for her mom's work."

"Well, there were years where she couldn't give her art away, so my Mom is taking all her new popularity in stride," Willa says jauntily.

Hayden raises her eyebrows, but quickly recovers, pretending to adjust one of the several gold chains layered around her neck. Her disdain for anything or anyone poor is so reflexive she can't control it. Wait till she finds out the truth about you, you think. She'll probably request a room transfer!

"Well, nice to meet you," Hayden says with the barest chill in her voice. Her high society link to Willa has been slightly weakened. She flashes a final icy smile and disappears with her friends into her single.

As soon as she disappears, the three of you exchange one look and burst into smiles, shaking your heads.

"We have two jam-packed days ahead before classes start on Monday," Casey says, nodding her head toward her room. "I think I'll try to finish unpacking."

"Me too," you agree.

You, Willa and Casey spend the 90 minutes till lights out hanging up your clothes, putting away sweaters, and arranging toiletries and school supplies. Your room looks spare, but you love it anyway. You're glad you brought pictures of you and Emily to tack up on your bulletin board. You'll have to see if there's an art poster you like at the school store, you think with a yawn as you climb into bed. Or maybe you can get a piece of Willa's overflow?

You had planned to lie awake in the dark, your favorite hour, to review your day. But life is changing quickly. And less than a minute after your head hits the pillow, you are fast asleep.

The next morning, a Saturday, kicks off with assembly in the school chapel at 8 AM. You walk over with Casey and Willa after a quick breakfast in the dining hall. There isn't a parent or limo anywhere, just faculty and students. This is what school will feel like on a regular day, you think, looking around.

As soon as you enter the magnificent Gothic Revival chapel, you get the same volcanic jolt of electricity you did the day before, when the airport shuttle van crossed onto school grounds. You look around. The same loud sound of rushing water temporarily drowns out the din of 320 chattering students and 84 faculty.

Casey frowns at you in concern. "Are you okay? You look pale."

"I'm okay," you answer trying to cover up your weirdo ways. "Isn't this place amazing?"

She nods in agreement.

"Anybody would have to admit that it's dazzling," Willa agrees, staring at all the gleaming carved wood.

"Except maybe Hayden," Casey cracks, and you all laugh. "Murdoch's bathroom at home is nicer than this."

You steer into a nearby pew. Just as you take your seats, a handsome woman in a purple tweed skirt and white silk blouse walks to the lectern near the altar in front. As she faces her audience, the chatter subsides to a low murmur and then, within five seconds, to total silence.

"Good morning, and welcome," the woman begins, smiling broadly, "to the first assembly of the new school year. My name is Eleanor Acheson, I am the Sixth Form Dean, and this is my show."

Several girls let out whoops and someone yells, "Go Ellie!"

"I'd like to express a special welcome to our new girls from all the faculty and staff here at Trumbull Woodhouse. We are delighted to have you here. You all have two very full days ahead so I will keep my remarks this morning brief."

With this she puts on some reading glasses and pulls out a small ivory paper. "Everyone should have gotten a schedule for today and tomorrow in their white registration packet yesterday. If you did not, or if you were a late arrival last night, those materials can be picked up in the Dean's Offices in the Wilberforce Building behind the Student Center any time this morning. This assembly will be followed immediately by meetings in your Dorms to go over school rules and procedures. Attendance is mandatory."

She looks up over her bi-focals and stares at some girls near the front. "Amanda, Susan, I think you might both benefit from a refresher in that department." Several girls laugh at her inside joke. You can see a shy-looking girl in the front pew blush bright pink.

"Uniforms will be on sale all day in the Student Annex," she continues. She pauses wickedly before adding, "Go early for the best selection." Several girls groan.

"Please make sure to go to the Counting House to arrange your account if your parents have not yet done so. There are team try-outs for Soccer, Field Hockey, Cross Country and Archery going on throughout the day. Please consult your schedule or the schedule in the Rotunda. Last but not least, you may pickup your laptop in the tent behind this building beginning at 11 this morning. You must bring your voucher with you to do so, no exceptions." She turns to a younger woman sitting nearby, "Is that it?" The woman hops up to whisper something in the Dean's ear.

"Right. There is some lost luggage that has been delivered to the Dean's offices. You can pick it up any time until 4:00 this afternoon," she adds.

In the middle of Dean Acheson's last sentence, the shrill tone of a pipe key in C rings out and suddenly, singing voices emerge from among the crowd of students. The singers rise from their places and begin walking toward the front of the room. Your jaw drops and your eyes bulge in amazement. You don't know much about music, but you know *a capella* – voice only without any instruments – is the hardest way to sing. These girls are so good, they sound like professionals. There are eleven of them in all. They start with the school song, and segue, without missing a beat, into the Cyndi Lauper song "Girls Just Wanna Have Fun." Casey leans in to whisper, "Those are the Chanticleers. A singing society here at Trumbull."

"You have to get tapped in by a girl who's already a member to even try out," Willa adds. "My mom was a member when she went here, which is how I know. You have to prepare five songs and draw on the spot which one you'll sing at the audition. Then, the next night, the Chanticleers go from dorm to dorm and serenade their new members. The girls accept by coming down and joining the group to go get the next girl and then they all go out for pizza in town. Sometime later is the induction ceremony where they're sworn to secrecy and taught secret chants and songs." Willa is an animated storyteller. She changes her tone and flashes her hands like she's telling a ghost story. "Only a couple of girls per class are picked."

The Chanticleers finish just as Willa does. The entire chapel breaks out in loud applause and several upperclass girls let out loud whoops. Dean Acheson makes a final announcement.

"Remember that there will be lunch directly following Convocation tomorrow at 11:00. Assembly dismissed."

The entire chapel rises to its feet. You, Casey, and Willa head back to Rose House and plunk down on a comfy chintz covered couch in the common area. Hayden comes in shortly, takes one cold look at you, and marches to sit as far away as possible. You feel yourself shrinking down in your seat, as Lily Mitchell calls the dorm meeting to order.

"Girls, may I have your attention please?" she says mildly. She doesn't have to yell to get people to listen. Everyone who is still standing and chatting reluctantly breaks up their cliques and stacks themselves on chairs and couches, sits cross-legged on floor pillows, and sprawls out on the overlapping rugs covering the hardwood floor. You count 24 girls in all. Someone at breakfast said that Rose House was one of the larger dorms. The din of whispering and chitchat dies out. "Thank you," Lily continues. "We have a lot of ground to cover, but we'll give you a chance at the end to ask questions or talk about anything that's on your mind," she reassures the group.

Lily pulls out a folder and flips it open. She rattles off a list of rules that could have wrapped around the room three times. "Attendance at all meals and all classes is mandatory for Third Form. You must sign into and out of the dorm every single time, no exceptions. Even if it is only for five minutes. As third formers, you must be checked into your dorm by 9 PM each night and lights must be out at 10 PM." A wave of grumbling swells from the group. Lily can't help but smile at the wave of discontent.

"There is no smoking anywhere on campus. Ever." She pauses and looks around the room at the wide eyes, rosy cheeks, and pimply faces of her young charges. Her tone grows stern, "But I don't think any of my girls need reminding of that, right?" she says as a warning, not a question. She waits until she has made eye contact with each girl in the room and then goes on reading from her list. "There is a zero tolerance policy for alcohol or drugs on campus. If you need to take prescription drugs, you must register them with Gordon and me, and we will dispense them to you as needed." She puts down the folder and adlibs. "And I don't think I need to remind you, but I will just in case. There is no lying, stealing, or cheating. Period." She nods decisively and hands the folder to Gordon. They exchange a smile that would melt your heart and send their talk show ratings through the roof, if they had one.

"Oh, sure. Give me the unsavory part," he says jokingly. "My wife has given me the dreaded job of going over the consequences in the unlikely event that you break any of these rules. Depending on the degree of the violation and the surrounding circumstances, of course, you will receive a one week suspension for your first infraction. A second violation will result in expulsion." A collective gasp sucks all of the air out of the room for a moment. "A grade average of a C or lower puts you in what we here at TW deem the danger zone, so you will lose off-campus privileges until you can bring it back up to at least C+. Also, you'll be required to see a tutor and attend Sunday study hall." He closes the folder and looks over at Lily.

"Okay, girls, the floor is yours. Ask away," she announces.

"And remember, there are no stupid questions. Only stupid girls who don't ask questions, fearing they'll look stupid," Gordon booms, chuckling deeply from his belly at his own joke.

A few girls raise their hands. The first question is about going off campus.

"Third Form girls are required to stay on campus for the first three weeks of school except for away sports events with their teams. This is to help everyone settle in to their life here. It is a policy that was arrived at through trial and error over many generations of girls. Believe me, it goes very quickly, and then normal off-campus permissions apply. Next."

"What about homework after lights out?" another girl asks.

"The school thinks adequate sleep is critical to academic achievement, so it's discouraged. But exceptions can be made with permission," Gordon replies.

Then, just as Lily launches into a lengthy explanation about the guidelines regarding dorm decorating in response to a girl who wants to bring a signed Chagall drawing, you're worst nightmare begins to come true.

A shimmer.

Someone is writing again on the crunchy page in sparkling gold ink. Each stroke of the pen is a river of light that dances on the page as if it were alive. The woman's hand is forming the letters of your name! You hear chant-

ing in the distance from somewhere far in the back of an enormous room. You try to make out the words, but they are singing in a foreign language filled with strange vowels. Latin or maybe Greek. Then it grows faint.

Your shimmer ends and the common room comes back into focus. Your eyes dart around the room, but everyone's attention is on the mousy girl with shiny hair from Illinois. She's asking about Mount Demetria, one of the three mountains that border the northern edge of campus. The same ones you can see from your dorm room window. You notice Lily stiffen a bit when she asks.

"Mount Demetria and most of Arcadia Mountain are strictly off limits to students. Those areas have never been properly mapped and are extremely wild. For your own safety, you are limited to the 458 acres that comprise the core of the campus. It's the area inside the thick dotted line on the official school map. Does everyone have one?" Lily asks, holding up a sample and pointing. "This permitted area includes most of Trumbull Hill, should you feel the urge to take a hike. The trails are well marked and worn."

"But why?" the girl asks in frustration. "I don't get it," she says defiantly.

"It's just one of the rules," Gordon cuts in.

"I heard girls have tried to sneak up Mount Demetria, but no one has gotten close," someone shouts from the back of the room.

"They say there's an ancient brick wall at the base that's impossible to get around," another girl adds.

A growing buzz rises from the girls as they twitter about various rumors they've heard. And like a faulty game of telephone, the information is getting as discombobulated as the girls who are passing it along.

"What about a monster?" another girl asks, sitting up from her pillow.

"Girls, girls," Lily says again. Déjà vu. "The school is not here to torture you," she begins. "If they make a rule about not going on Mount Demetria, I assure you there is a good reason for it. And sometimes you have to just trust in the system," she says, as if that's a good explanation to something this juicy.

When are adults going to learn "because I said so" is not a real answer?

"In the past, girls have tried to go up there, and gotten caught. They received demerits and some even got suspended. So unless you want to spend your free time doing table wipes, cleaning the dorms, working in the gardens around the admissions offices, or explaining to your parents why you have to come home in the middle of the school year, I suggest you stay away from Mount Demetria," Gordon finishes for her. "Any other questions?"

"What about laundry?" Casey asks.

"Right. Glad you asked. Laundry is picked up weekly on Wednesday from the front hall. Put anything you want washed in water in one of the blue cotton laundry bags hanging in your closet along with a laundry form. Forms are available online We also keep a supply in our office. Laundry is returned Friday by 5:00."

"And dry cleaning?" someone else chimes in. You recognize the voice. It's Hayden of course. She probably dry cleans her undies.

"Pick up and drop off is at the school store," Lily replies.

"Are we allowed to have pets?" a pretty girl with a thick

brown braid asks.

"No unfortunately," Lily responds. "Not even goldfish."

"But we're thinking of getting a labradoodle," Gordon announces.

Several girls plead with your dorm parents to get the dog. And with that the meeting is adjourned.

You, Willa and Casey have already decided to head straight over to the Annex behind the student center where uniforms are for sale. You only have $366 that you managed to save up from your babysitting gigs over the summer, and hopefully this will cover the basics. At the door, an elderly woman who was also serving food in the dining hall hands out a printed flyer with a list of Uniform Guidelines. The school recommends at least three kilts, five white button down shirts, two blazers, and two cardigans.

"What's 'Dress Uniform' mean?" you ask.

"Unadulterated," Willa answers.

"No accessories or jewelry, white stockings or knee socks, and flat dress shoes," Casey elaborates. "Dress uniform is required at all special school events, like Convocation tomorrow. Everyday uniforms can be accessorized."

"Can they ever," Willa says.

You continue to read.

"Uniforms are required at all times on campus except at night after dinner and on weekends after class."

Inside the warehouse-like Annex, it is total mayhem. Rows of long tables piled high with shirts, skirts, and jackets line the perimeter of the room. In the center are check-out tables manned by more Trumbull staff. And everywhere in between are girls, girls, girls. It looks and sounds like back stage at a fashion show as they strip down, try on, swap up, and check out. You spot three tables marked "Pre-Owned," that are untouched and unattended. And you know that's where you'll find the majority of your wardrobe. Used usually means cheaper, so you tell Casey and Willa you're heading over there. To your surprise, they come with you.

"I love anything recycled. Go green!" Casey says thrusting her fist in the air.

"They're not used, they're vintage. It gives them character," is Willa's spin on it.

You can't tell if they are just being good friends or if they would buy used uniforms even if you were not there. But you really don't care. Your heart fills up with appreciation for your new friends and you actually enjoy sifting through the hand-me-downs for your new clothes. By the time you are ready to check out, you have carefully chosen one new and one used kilt, a blazer that looks new, and three shirts that are as good as new. Your total comes to just under $300, so they will have to do for now.

You, Casey, and Willa drop your uniform purchases at Rose House and approach the giant steel grey fort that has sprung up overnight behind the student center. "Trumbull Technology Tent" is printed in Times New Roman, 1000 point font on a white banner above the door, and the front face and sides of the tarpaulin walls have been painted to look like a desktop computer.

Well, they're not so much doors as they are flaps, but they do the trick. It's a mirage of modernity erected among the old-fangled dorms and picturesque cottages, about as unthinkable as the piece of paper you are clutching inside the right pocket of your shorts. It's your laptop voucher, a rectangular strip of construction paper signed by the Third Form Dean that's worth about three grand. It entitles you to one brand-spanking new MacBook Pro with all the fixins', and until you hand it over to one of the four-eyed techies in this tent, someone is going to have to pry it out of your cold, dead hand.

Casey and Willa have theirs too. Willa tucked hers inside her bra. Casey's voucher is three-hole punched in her Orientation Binder that rests in the crook of her arm. If you hadn't met her M.D. parents, you'd swear she was constructed, packaged, and shipped from the stock room of The Container Store.

"Good afternoon, girls. I'm Bailey," a gangly, freckle-faced guy with a clipboard greets you as you step inside. You give him the quick once-over. He can't be more than sixteen. He's bobbing his head to the electronica music pulsing from wireless speakers dangling from the ceiling.

"Don't worry, I come in peace," he says holding up his right hand, his palm facing you. "I grew up with five sisters, so I've learned to mimic the ways of your kind for my own survival."

You have to smile, but he can see his humor doesn't go over as well with Casey and Willa.

"Oooo-K. Tough crowd. If you'll just take a place in line under the first letter of your last name, we'll get you laptopped."

"The only thing worse than a plain vanilla computer nerd is a Trekkie Techie," Casey mumbles to you before you are forced to split up.

As you stand in line, you catch yourself bopping to the beat of the music, staring blankly at the girl's teetering head in front of you. The rhythm is infectious, and it's wriggled into the brains of the other girls standing in line around you. Here we are, you think, the leaders of the future, twenty-three bobbleheads in a row. When you get to the front of the line, you see a life-size circuit board whirring with volunteers on the other side of the long tables. An older man with hairy arms and little tufts of hair sprouting from his nostrils and ears smiles up at you from his seat.

"Voucher, please," he says in a polite but no-nonsense manner. You carefully press the paper into his hand; he's already reaching under the table for your new baby. He snaps it out of its box, and places it in your outstretched arms, along with a nylon carrying bag. You cradle it awkwardly, not wanting to bruise or break it.

"Now take this and go to the Add-On table over there," he says, scribbling on another slip of paper. "Ask for Anupa. Tell her you want package 162. Okay? Next," he calls out, already looking past you at the next laptop mom-to-be. You take each step towards the table carefully, as if the ground under your feet can't be trusted, not with this precious cargo. You gaze down at your new laptop. Is this beautiful machine really yours? No one to kick you off. No egg timer buzzing annoyingly next to it to time your use. No ice-cream fingers to smudge the keys. It's yours. All yours! You and Emily used to go to the Apple store at the mall and spend all day playing on the demos. She would start a bonfire if she saw you now.

"Hi, are you Anupa?" you ask a girl with long black braids and almond colored skin. Her magenta dress is on fire against her smooth, dark skin. But this girl is young, so young she could be your suitemate.

"All day," she says pushing a stick of pale blue gum into her mouth and taking your slip. She shakes her head and rips up the paper, little white squares raining down onto the table. "Lemme guess, Tom over there told you to tell me you need package 162," she says dryly.

"Uh, yes. He did," you say, your confusion growing.

"I'm gonna let you in on a little secret about Tom," she says leaning in on her elbows. "All that hair has taken root at the base of his brain and grown like weed. It's cutting off his ability to think," she says lowering herself back down. "Are you in Greek or Latin?" she asks snatching your laptop from your arms. You lurch forward but then realize it's in good hands.

"Ancient Greek."

"Okay. Which Bio-lab are you in?" She already has your laptop fired up and is loading software at lightening speed.

"Section one."

"Don't worry, we're almost done." Her fingers are a streak of skin on the keyboard. "Who do you have for Pre-Calculus?"

"Uh...Peirce!" you say, relieved you remembered his name.

Her head snaps up. "Me too!" she wails. "I don't know about you, but I better have enjoyed my previous life, cause that's some serious Karma."

"Wait, you're a student?" you say.

"Yeah, I'm a Third Former." She sees your face buckling in on itself in confusion. "Oh, this?" she says spinning her hand around the tent. "I'm just helping out today. It's part of my work-study. And half these guys couldn't find a data stream protocol with a flashlight and manual." You have no idea what she's talking about, but you get the gist and laugh anyway. "Except for Bailey over there by the door. He knows his stuff. He's not much older than we are. He goes to the local public high school, but he won a full scholarship to the summer MIT gifted program. " She says with a nod as if that tells you everything you need to know about that.

"I'm in Rose House. How about you?" you say as she slides your laptop back into its bag and hands it over.

"Shut up. Rose House? Third Floor." She says rising from her seat, her bright eyes going from fern to tea green.

"Were you at the rules meeting this morning?" you ask. You don't remember seeing her.

"Yes, sitting in back," she answers.

"Maybe you can come by later? I'm in 2B," you say shyly. It's your first friend invite outside the suite. But you feel more connected to her in fifteen seconds than you do with most people after a year.

"I have to be here all day. And I'm on computer lab duty before Convocation tomorrow," she says plainly. "Maybe after lunch?" As if it's the most mundane thing to be fourteen and smarter at something than everyone else. "I'll definitely come find you at some point," she says happily. "And we can always meet outside the gate of Hell," she says, "otherwise knows as Pre-Calculus with Peirce."

"Okay, see you soon," you say as you go to find Casey and Willa. And you mean it. You can't wait to hang out with Anupa.

You take your Macbook home to your room, and plug it in. Before you know it, an hour has passed and it's time to go again. The dorm's WiFi makes it easy to waste time and hard to part with your new baby. But your packet of mail yesterday included a reminder to come to The Counting House some time during the day on Saturday to "arrange your accounts." It's time to face the music and JV Soccer try-outs immediately thereafter.

You bring along the entire contents of your piggy bank — all $66 of it left over after purchasing your uniform. This meager amount will have to last you through the fall. Tuition covers room and board, meals, books, a new laptop, and basic supplies, so you should be okay. But you make a special mental note to ask your advisor Elizabeth Wilmington when you meet later today if you could work for the school or do odd jobs for the faculty during breaks and holidays to earn a little extra cash.

You consult your school map, and begin to understand why Regan had plasticized hers. You've already folded and refolded it so many times, the creases are starting to wear thin. After fifteen minutes of walking in circles, you finally find it. Part of the trouble was that the building is not what you expected. In fact, it's not really a building at all. The Counting House is an old converted barn. It's only when you get up close that you can see that the green patina roof is because it's copper. How many barns that you know have etched glass windows and floors made from the mahogany from old whaling ships (a piece of Trumbull Trivia you read on the small plaque near the door)? Despite its quaint name and old-fashioned exterior, there's some serious business going on inside. You'll learn that The Counting House functions as Trumbull Woodhouse's very own bank and charge center.

Mrs. Winthorpe, the official Bursar, gives you a peculiar look when you dump your dollars onto the counter and ask her to apply it to your account. "You want to deposit this?" she asks squinting over her wire-rimmed glasses and down her pointy nose. You know your nest egg is tiny, but did she have to make you feel insignificant too?

"I was assuming you would want to make a withdrawal," she continued.

"Withdrawal?" you reply. "I think you have me confused with another girl. I don't have any money in my student account. That's why I brought this," you say gesturing to your crumpled cash. Her left eyebrow shoots up into a pointed peak to match her nose. She's not used to a challenge, especially when she's telling a student they have more money than they think they do. Her eyes dart from you to her computer screen. The bright light from the screen casts a blue tint on her ashen skin as she clicks through windows you can't see. She must've found what she was looking for because her thin eyebrow returns to a flat, black line above her eye. "Your account has a balance of $3332.78, after deducting your payment for the shuttle and fall activities fee," she says with a hint of satisfaction.

You laugh out loud. You can't help it. You? Over $3,000? That's not just a mistake, that's a joke.

"I'm sorry," you cover your mouth with your hand for a moment to compose yourself. You remove it, giving her a polite smile. "It's just that I've never had that much money in my entire life. Even if you added up all fourteen years! I think I'd know if I did."

The thought of you having so much money makes you burst out laughing. But she's not amused. Without taking her eyes off of you, she slides off her stool and moves towards the back of the barn where a giant matrix of little wooden drawers covers one wall. Something about the way she sidles down the aisle of desks tells you she doesn't like having to leave her post, and it's rare that anyone makes her. Her long skirt and tan leather shoes that squish with each step make her look older than she is. She runs her hand down the rows of drawers, not bothering to look at the rectangular plaques that label each one. She knows where she's going. And when she gets there, she wrenches the drawer open, flips through the cards inside, pulls one out halfway, and returns it to the line. The drawer slides back with a soft thud. She makes her way back to her stool. Her eyes trained on you the entire time.

Mrs. Winthorpe may be good with numbers and fast on the keyboard, but she's not setting any land speed records. You've counted to ten hippopotamus three times by the time she reaches you.

"Okay, Miss. As hard as it may be for you to believe, it's true. $3332.78, just like your electronic file says."

"What?! But how? I mean, who would've put it there? Can you check for me, please?" you plead. Mrs. Winthorpe lets out a sigh that would blow over an elephant and slips off her stool for the second time today. This time she disappears behind a partition. Your mind is racing. David and Karen haven't even called to check on you. There's no way they would – or even could – be so generous. You don't remember your financial aid letter saying anything about spending money. And this is so much money! Mrs. Winthorpe reappears and her journey back seems even longer this time. You are ready to burst with anticipation.

"You're going to have to speak to your advisor about that. I'm not at liberty to say," she says after taking her sweet time repositioning herself on her stool. "But it is your money, regardless of who put it there."

Pop! Something inside you bursts. An odd cocktail of frustration, excitement, confusion, and disbelief and hope floods your veins. You feel lightheaded.

"You will receive a weekly allowance of $75 in your mailbox every Friday. That's when all the allowances are disbursed. I can deposit this cash for you," she adds, with a sweeping gesture at the bills on her counter, "but I recommend you keep at least $30 for the vending machines in the dorm or The Snack Shack. When you start leaving campus, you might need more." You nod, still stunned by the news. She nods and sweeps all but $30 into a white envelope, writes your name on it and places it in the bin marked "Deposits." She pushes a clipboard in front of you and hands you a pen. You spend the next few minutes filling out a series of forms to establish your account and set a password. You pass the clipboard back to her and turn to leave. You could go back to the uniform room to get a cardigan, and you could use a new pair of shoes, like the ones you saw at the Nest. And a new lip gloss. And maybe a new mascara because your old one is dried out. The list is already forming.

The high from news of your windfall mini-fortune doesn't last long. It's kicked, tripped, and elbowed out of you during two hours of JV soccer try-outs. The only buzz you have now is the one rattling in your ears, thanks to a strategic side-swipe from a Fourth Former that took you out at the knees.

These girls are insane.

And insanely good.

Their footwork is dazzling and their dribbling unstoppable. It seems like everyone's a playmaker. You're still pulling blades of grass and bits of dirt from between your teeth as you stand midfield planning your next attack.

You were never a star on Hatterly middle school's soccer team, but you were one of its best wings. You even scored the winning goal against Bishopville last fall. Normally playing soccer is a time you can shut everything out and get in the zone. When you're on the field, it's just you and the ball. There's no room in your head for grades, missing parents, or even shimmers. So it seemed like a good idea to try out for the team. But after an afternoon of impossible passes and unthinkable goals, you are convinced these girls have eyes in the back of their heads.

"Shweeeet!" the whistle blows signaling game on. You start to run up the field, covering a girl who is Beckham in braces. At this point, you're no longer sure if you want to make the Junior Varsity team. Maybe a nice, no-pressure position on the intramural club team would be more fun? And less painful. Finally the head coach blasts the quick twills, signaling that try-outs are over.

"Thank you ladies for all the hard work!" she hollers. "Team selection will be posted by dinner tomorrow on the message board in the Rotunda. You can also find it on the JV Soccer forum on The Field. Good work!"

You are bent in half, gasping for breath.

"Heading back to the room?" Casey asks. She's caked with sweat and dirt too, but hardly winded. Casey played for a select league team in Bar Harbor. She'll make JV for sure.

"Nah. I have to meet with my advisor," you answer. You glance at your wrist. 4:27. You have three minutes to get there. "Oh my gosh! I didn't realize we practiced so long. I gotta run or I'll be late."

You wave to Casey and rush off across campus to the little cottage near the edge of the woods where Elizabeth Wilmington lives. You are a little nervous to meet her after Regan's reaction yesterday. And legend or not, you'd rather be showering off than shifting nervously in your sweaty soccer cleats on her wraparound porch. Despite the tubby tabby cat napping on the steps and beds of blooming dahlias and foxglove lining the walkway, there is an eerie vibe emanating from this place. The glow of the green porch light isn't helping things either. Just as you raise your hand to knock, a majestic, white-haired woman opens the door.

"Welcome, my dear. I've been expecting you." She has a brilliant smile that illuminates the darkened doorway. She shakes your hand with a powerful grip, her skin smooth as velvet. She turns her body to the side and sweeps her arm out and around to invite you in. As you step into her foyer, she gently clicks the door closed behind you. There is a familiar smell of incense and flower petals, like the one you smelled in the van when you first crossed the campus gates.

"What is that smell?" you ask as you sniff the air.

"Let's see, that is a mixture of bergamot, magnolia, tuberose, and sage. Do you like it?"

"I love it. I've smelled it before..." you trail off, suddenly embarrassed. You didn't mean to say that last part because it was during one of those shimmer waves that have been washing over you. You bite the inside of your top lip to keep from slipping up again.

"You have?" she asks curiously but not at all surprised.

"Well, something similar anyway." You put your hands behind your back and cross the first two fingers on your right and left hands. One side for lying and the other hoping she won't ask any more details. You certainly can't tell her about the surge of electricity and strange smells you experienced in the van. She would think you're crazy. And what if she started asking questions? You may have to tell her about your heightened senses, the surges of heat and pins and needles that come at least twice an hour since you arrived at Trumbull Woodhouse, and maybe even your shimmers. Nope, you learned to keep a lid on that can of worms when you were six.

As she leads you into her living room, her rich, steady voice lingers in the air behind her.

"Did you know that if you burn that specific recipe, it is supposed to bring you good luck within 24 hours?"

You shake your head no, but she can't see you with her back turned. She goes on anyway, "And if you substitute lavender for the tuberose, that combination is supposed to help you find true love." She glances back, her eyebrows arched expectantly over her hazel eyes. "But that may take a little longer." She is so regal and striking, she reminds you of a lioness.

"Why don't you have a seat, and I'll get us some tea and biscuits," she says motioning to a plush velvet mushroom-colored sofa and two arm chairs gathered around a large coffee table. You choose a spot on the sofa facing the mottled stone fireplace. Two more cats emerge from their hiding places under each chair to investigate you. They look at you with cocked heads, like they don't often see strange visitors.

"You'll have to get used to me," you tell them.

One with little black stripes running down his soft brown fur slips between your feet and rubs against your leg.

"You're not allergic to cats, right?" Elizabeth Wilmington says. It sounds more like she is telling you than asking you. Almost as if she already knows. You shake your head no and reach down to stroke the cat's back.

"Bees. Not cats," she says under her breath on her way to the kitchen. Your head snaps up. You are allergic to bees. You scratch your brain to remember if you listed that fact on one of the eight trillion forms the school sent over the summer. You must've put it on the medical questionnaire. But still, Elizabeth has done her homework.

It's a small cottage, so you can hear every clink and cupboard door as Elizabeth moves around her kitchen. You could easily talk to her while she's in there without moving from the couch, but you stay quiet and follow her lead. She's nice, but very formal, and seems like the kind of woman that has impeccable manners and expects the same of you. You are petrified of making a social misstep. Instead, you look around the elegantly decorated living room while you wait. Every inch of wallspace is covered with paintings and drawings. Your eye wanders across the wall and you gasp when you see a small painting of a calla lily in close-up, not more than eight inches square. It is showcased in an simple gold frame with its own special high beam light. There's another painting, sitting on a small easel on an antique table, that calls to you. This one is larger, the portrait of a young dark-haired woman in a Mexican dress staring straight at you intently. A small bluebird pulls a loose thread from the shawl she is wearing and is flying away toward a window.

You remember Willa telling you that Elizabeth's art collection is famous. Her parents even made a special visit to Elizabeth's house last spring when she visited TW in person. You study each canvas displayed under a tiny spotlight and try to decipher the artists' signatures. Kahlo, O'Keefe, There's a charming trio of paintings in blues and greens of the same narrow garden with a stone fountain, each slightly different. You make out the artist's name Bartlett. The names don't mean anything to you. But you decide to look up a couple on the Internet when you get back to your dorm.

Elizabeth returns and sets down a tray with a teapot, three cups and saucers, and a silver milk pitcher and sugar bowl. The cats retreat back under the chairs. They've decided you are neither threatening enough nor entertaining enough to keep them from their naps.

"Do you like art?" she asks, noticing you study the paintings.

"Yes, but I don't know much about it," you say.

"It's my passion," she says smiling mysteriously, pouring a

cup of tea. "That and ancient history."

She hands you the cup of tea with milk and no sugar. When Elizabeth said "biscuits," you were imagining biscuits and gravy, which seemed a little weird with tea. But these aren't biscuits, they're cookies! Delicious little shortbread cookies infused with orange. You wait for her to offer you the plate and remember to nibble, not bite, from the side of the cookie. The granules of sugar dissolve in your mouth. Yummy! And after your exhausting soccer practice, you could eat the whole plate in two bites. But you place the cookie on your saucer and sip your tea. Elizabeth sits back with her cup and saucer and studies you. Her stare is unnerving and penetrating, like that woman's gaze on the airplane. It feels like she's reading your thoughts. But that's crazy, right?

"Is someone else coming?" you ask, trying to fill the silence and dispel the suspicion. Her eyes move slowly to the empty third cup and saucer still on the tray.

"I thought I'd set a place for Luck, just in case it decides to show up," she says, a little smile tugging at the corners of her mouth. She has a trace of an accent that you don't recognize. "So tell me, dear, how did you choose Trumbull Woodhouse?" Elizabeth wastes no time.

"Um...well, it chose me I guess, really. I mean it was my first choice all along..." you gulp your tea to buy some time. You're not sure how much you want to reveal. But if she knew about the bees, surely she's read your entire file. So you plow ahead.

"The school gave me a full scholarship." You pause again and breathe deeply. "And I needed somewhere I could unpack my bag for good. Where I wouldn't have to worry about getting sent away again."

"Yes, I'm aware of the Donovans' decision to terminate your

foster relationship. I'm not sure if you were informed, but we've been working with the State over the summer. They have agreed that I will be your legal guardian during your course here. Technically, that means signing forms and what not. But more importantly, I am here to steward you and support you. That is, if that is okay with you." She looks at you, her eyebrows shooting up into arches again.

"I had no idea, but I'm okay with that," you say, trying to process it.

"Good. I know the reticence that comes from not having anyone you can count on doesn't dissolve overnight with a welcome packet and a uniform. We should keep an ongoing dialogue about how you feel. The experiences you're having." She pauses. "Anything unusual that occurs..."

You nod, still letting it sink in that Elizabeth is your new guardian.

"So how are you feeling now that you're here?" she asks cutting to the quick.

"Okay, I guess. It's been a whirlwind of rules, times, names, hometowns. When I woke up this morning, I checked my pillow to see if any of the new information had fallen out during the night." You laugh nervously.

"So no unexpected feelings? Signs that this was the right decision? Regrets?" She asks searching your face, but for what you cannot tell. For a moment, it feels like she knows about the surges and sensations you've been having. The words rush from your brain to your throat. You almost blurt them out, but you bite your lip again and they sit on the tip of your tongue. You're just being paranoid.

"No, no regrets. But...well, there is one thing."

"Yes? Go on," Elizabeth says eagerly. She leans forward ever so slightly.

"It's just that I haven't told anyone about being a foster kid...you know, an orphan," you say hesitantly.

Elizabeth nods, settling back into her chair. "I understand," she replies. "It is an intimate detail, but not one you should be afraid to share."

"Have you walked around this campus in the last couple of days? It's bad enough I don't have the latest bag or the right shoes or bracelets. I can only imagine what they'd think if they knew I didn't have rich parents. Or any parents..."

"What do you say when people ask?"

"I don't lie or anything," you assure her. "I just kind of talk about 'home' and try to avoid anything too specific. I've referred to Karen and David, so some girls probably got the impression they were my parents. And I didn't bother to correct them. But that can only go on so long. And besides, it feels weird. Like I'm hiding something."

"Everyone deserves a fresh start," she observes, "And there are many girls here who have things about their lives they would rather keep secret. Take your time and do what feels right. But I hope that one day you grow comfortable enough here to be completely yourself. And not have to hide anything."

She seems to emphasize that last word in particular. It presses into your ear, and she holds your gaze to cement the word onto your brain so you can't forget it.

There is one other question you are dying to ask. And since she already knows your life story, there's no reason to sugar coat it. "Can I ask you about something?" you begin.

"By all means," she replies.

"Do you know about the money on my student account?"

"Yes, of course," she nods.

"Who put it there?" you ask. "It's not a part of my scholarship, is it?"

"Once classes begin, you'll see how rigorous the academics are here, and we didn't want financial concerns distracting you. So The Artemis Group stepped forward, as they do from time to time, to supplement the scholarship of a student in need who may not otherwise reach her full potential," she explains. But her tone is odd, like she's reading from a brochure. You know she's formal, but you can tell there's something she's tiptoeing around. And who's the "we" she refers to?

"The Artemis Group?" you repeat.

"It's a group of Trumbull Woodhouse alumni who are in prominent positions in society and can afford to come together and give back to the school who helped put them there."

She speaks slowly and deliberately, choosing her words carefully like someone picking fruit at the grocery store. "Please let me know if it's enough."

You almost spit out your tea! Enough?

"It's more than enough, thank you. And thank you so much for everything you're doing for me."

She nods graciously, and goes on to ask a few more questions about your interests and hobbies, and where you've traveled which is not far.

"Well, I can see it's growing dark out," she says abruptly looking over at the bay window. The floor to ceiling thick, stained glass is a work of art itself, with every color of the rainbow. The opaque lead glass and dark colors make it impossible for you to tell whether it's day or night out there, but Elizabeth obviously can. "We should get you home in time to wash up for dinner." She says rising to her feet. "I hope the biscuits didn't spoil your appetite."

"Oh, I could have eaten the whole box after soccer try-outs," you blurt out.

For the first time Elizabeth laughs.

As she leads you to the door, she pauses for a moment. "Have you spoken with Chloe LeFleur yet?"

You shrug and shake your head.

"No, why?"

She purses her lips in disappointment. "That's unfortunate. You might seek her out. The two of you have more in common than you think."

You feel uneasy, as though you just failed a test you didn't know you were taking until it was over. You try to shake off this feeling as you step out of her little cocoon and onto her porch bathed in green light. She was right, the harvest moon is rising in the sky and the wind has picked up a little making the air chilly. You wish you had your blazer.

"It was a pleasure to finally meet in person," she says. "I'm so very glad you've come to the school."

You nod. "Thank you for tea," you reply, feeling somewhat awkward still.

You shake hands, alarmed by her powerful grip again, and turn to tiptoe down the steps. Once the house is just a spec of green light behind you and you're sure Elizabeth can no longer see, you sprint the rest of the way home.

You get back to Rose House in time for a quick shower before heading to dinner with Casey and Willa.

"How was your meeting with your Advisor?" Casey asks casually as you wait in the dining line for your made-to-order quesadillas.

"Okay, I guess," you say, not sure if that's how your really feel. "Actually, I'm still trying to decide. She's kind of intimidating, So it's not like it went badly, it just wasn't tons of fun," you add.

"See what I meant about her art collection?" Willa cuts in, stretching her swan neck over Casey's tray. "Her living room is like the Museum of Fine Arts. Did you see her Kara Walker?" Willa asks, now distracted by the bins of steaming rice and beans a staff member has just replaced. She shells out scoop after scoop onto her plate.

"I hate to admit it Wills," you reply, "but I wouldn't know it if I did."

You both laugh.

By the time you sit down with your Frisbee shaped tortillas stuffed with smoked chicken and jack cheese, your stomach has given up on growling and decided to eat itself. You wolf down not one but two entire quesadillas piled high with salsa and sour cream. That should show your stomach who's boss.

You don't have to worry about leaving room for popcorn or junior mints at the Saturday night movie, you're not going.

"What? Why not?" Casey asks concerned.

"I have a date with Sebastian. He's waiting for me in my room," you say sneakily.

"You've got a guy in your room!?" Casey cries in her best dining hall whisper, which may have well been said into a megaphone. You notice several heads near by perk up.

"No, that's what I've named my laptop," you laugh. "And yes, it was love at first sight for both of us, in case you were wondering."

Willa and Casey head to the movie and you walk back alone through the chilly and breezy September dark to your suite. You are head over heels for your new Mac boyfriend, and you are also dying to spend some time in The Field. All you were able to do earlier today was register with the name and password provided in your registration packet. With everyone tied up for at least two hours watching "Confessions of a Teenage Drama Queen" in the main theater, you'll be able to noodle around and check out other people's pages and read some of the forums. You are still figuring out how Trumbull Woodhouse works. And you know that The Field will have lots of clues.

You log in and hear the satisfying "plinks" of Field messages dropping in to your box. You've been invited to make friends with Casey, Willa, one of the Idaho cousins, and Anupa and to become a member of the Group called Rose House. You accept all five invitations and then insert a going-away disc of photos that Emily gave you to find a good one to post for your head shot. You are signing up for an open Group called This Week's Menus when someone knocks.

"Can I come in?" Anupa asks shyly, sticking her head in your door.

"Hey!" you cry. "Absolutely! Grab a seat. I'm just playing in The Field."

Anupa grins and perches on the edge of your bed since there isn't a second chair. Your room is so compact that this means she is looking right over your shoulder.

"Everything working alright?" she asks.

"It's perfect. My first own computer ever," you tell her, tracing the edge of the screen with your finger.

You can tell Anupa is surprised by this revelation. Her eyebrows snap up into little peaks pulling her jungle green-shaded eyelids with them. "Back in South Carolina I had to share," you explain. "We even had a timer. How lame is that!" you say rolling your eyes.

"About as lame as having to share bunk beds with your little sister until you were ten," Anupa laughs. "My parents thought it would bring us closer. But just because you sleep four feet above someone doesn't mean you're going to be best buddies." She shakes her head at the thought of her old bedroom. "Well, I'm the go to girl if you have any questions." she says affably.

Little reminder bells throng in your ears. Something's been bothering you since yesterday when you first heard about The Field and you learned about everything you'd been missing out on. At first you just blamed the spam filter on Karen's computer.

But there's no way that could be it, and you know it. You

used to check that spam file all the time in case there was a link to a YouTube video or a newspaper article Emily sent you. And you didn't have a problem getting any of the other e-mails from the school, and there were lots of those over the summer. They were on your favorites list. You're positive it wasn't Karen or even the devil child Mason because you changed your passwords weekly as a precaution. So how was it that your Field invitation never arrived? Anupa is just the person to ask.

"What do you know about sending group emails?" you ask.

"Everything. That's kiddie pool stuff. What's up? You need to send an email to a large number of people?" she asks rising to her feet.

"No, but I want to know how someone else might do it," you say. "Like how would the school send our class email? Like the invite to join The Field?"

"Simple. They have a surprisingly robust technology department here, thanks mostly to Bailey. It was a form-generated email with various fields to fill in so they could randomly assign temporary passwords and track them back through a database. There are 72 new Third formers and 23 other new girls in Fourth and Fifth Form, so they needed to send out 95 invites. They have their own mail server for security reasons. So they can send everything out themselves without using an outside service. And for a number that small it wouldn't be a big deal to send individually."

"So they could have accidentally omitted one?" you ask, almost hopefully.

"I doubt it. They would regression test to verify for something important like that. It's SOP." Anupa replies. She sees your eyebrows smash together in confusion. "Standard Operating Procedure."

"Got it," you say. You take a deep breath and let it out slowly through your nose. Hopefully the air will flush out the little specs of worry that are making your nose tingle. "So, how do you know so much?"

Anupa laughs and blushes. "I know enough to know I don't know nearly enough," she replies modestly. But she can tell you're not satisfied with her non-answer. "When I was younger, people always said to me, 'oh, Anupa you're so smart.' And they always said to my little sister, 'Pasha you're so pretty.' And that was it. And since the best thing about me was on the inside and hers was on the outside, she got all of the attention. I turned to my trusty computer who never turned away from me." She bats her eyelashes ironically, just in case things were getting a little too serious.

"What's your sister like?" you ask, trying to imagine the rest of Anupa's family.

"A crowd-pleasing brat. The parentals love that she studies and performs ancient Hindu dance. We grew up in Ann Arbor, but my parents are fresh off the boat from India. Well, not really, they just still act like it," she informs you. "They're pretty old-fashioned. They think computer technology is something for boys."

You shake your head in disbelief.

"My dad lived here for about four years before he sent for my mom, my sister and me. He stayed in a one-room studio with two other guys and worked three jobs to save up enough money. Can you believe that? I bet most of these girls' closets at home were bigger than his entire apartment! But now he owns the dry cleaners where he first ironed shirts. And my mom is a seamstress. She does all the alterations at the store. How's that for living the American Dream?"

Anupa is the first girl you've met at this school that wasn't born with a silver spoon in her mouth. She may not be an orphan, but you learn Anupa didn't have parents to move her in on the first day of school either. Lakshana and Ashok, her mom and dad, didn't want her coming to boarding school in the first place. They don't believe Anupa should be living outside their home until she marries the man they pick out for her. Her father barely spoke to her the last weeks before she left. But the reason they didn't travel with her was Pasha.

"The Golden Child had a performance back in Ann Arbor. When Pasha dances, the world stops, or at least for my parents," Anupa says with a mixture of acceptance and resentment. You feel sorry for Anupa. It had never occurred to you that the only thing worse than not having parents is having ones who love someone more than you.

"Wow, it's really brave that you stood up to them and came here," you say, admiring her more by the minute.

Anupa shrugs and smiles. "I think we're all pretty brave for coming here."

The information you gleaned from picking Anupa's brain gives you something to chew on for the rest of the night. And it's the first thing you think of when you wake up.

No matter how many times you run through it in your head, no matter which way you fold it or flip it over, you keep arriving at the same conclusion – someone somehow blocked your invite to The Field. You know it sounds crazy, so you didn't mention it to Anupa, not yet anyway. You're just making friends and don't want to come off like a paranoid Nancy Drew, smelling a rat with every click of the mouse. Even so, it bothers you a lot.

You try to turn your attention to other things as you get dressed for the convocation ceremony. It's a beautiful early fall day. The sky is a wide strip of clear blue stretching overhead. As you sit on your bed pulling on your white stockings, you say to yourself, "I am so lucky. I'm grateful to be here." And you are. It's not just the New England weather or your ridonculous new bank account, or even the crisp new uniform you're donning. You glance in the mirror for one last quick check and do a little curtsy, a modern-day Cinderella going to the ball.

On the way out of your dorm, you pass Lily, who is perched on a chair in the front hall. She keeps one eye her knitting, and the other eye on each girl as she leaves her room. Lily is on uniform watch.

"Remember, girls, it's Full Dress Uniform for an official school function," she sing songs up the stairs.

She sends several girls back to their rooms to remove jewelry, hair clips, shoes with a heel, or colored tights. It appears that "Full Dress" means "straight by the book." No sass. Even Wild Wild Willa, as Casey has started to call her, abides by the strictures, although with her homemade haircut, it's hard to take all the zing out of her appearance.

As you walk over to chapel, you notice that the only girl who seems to be able to push the envelope is Hayden. She wears the Trumbull Woodhouse standard issue plaid kilt, but it flatters her legs as if it was custom-made. On her, the perfectly appointed navy wool blazer with shiny gold buttons looks like a jacket off the pages of Vogue. And her "white shirt with collar," as the rule book requires, has a brilliant white ruffle two inches wider than anyone else's, popped to draw attention to her face. It frames her tawny skin and perfect golden hair like the petals of a flower. Instead of white stockings, she wears the way hotter alternate: white ankle socks. And as if that's not different enough, hers are made of fluffy angora with cotton lace along the tops.

You begrudgingly have to admit: the girl is a blonde bombshell. She's got the total package: knockout looks, sick fashion sense, and a perfect body, and she knows it too.

Your attention shifts when the chapel comes into view. It's

surrounded by bushels of exquisitely-dressed women, a knot of black sedans and limos, dozens of faculty members in full cap and gown regalia, and hundreds of members of this year's Trumbull Woodhouse student body. You pinch yourself again. Four brightly colored banners have been erected, two on either side of the chapel entrance. They're almost two stories tall and flap in the wind like sails making a brisk snapping sound. They are covered in schematic silhouettes of several animals and insects, including a badger, several bees, a swan and a goat!

"Wow, check out the gorgeous sashes that the faculty are rocking," Willa exclaims. "I want one!"

"Those tell you their degrees and the university where they received them," Casey informs you both. "You'll need to get your doctorate first, Willa," she says, patting Willa on the back.

"Almost all of the faculty have doctorates," Casey adds. "It's one of the things that make this place so good academically. Most of our profs could be teaching at colleges or universities if they wanted to."

"Then why do they teach here?" you ask.

"Some of them went here, so they want to come back to their alma mater," Casey says. "But that's not the only reason. Everyone knows it's the money. TW is famous for the highest faculty salaries of any secondary school in the nation. Higher than most universities. Plus free housing and full benefits."

"Jeez. They must have some serious donations," you speculate.

"They have an endowment," Casey adds informatively. "Trumbull's dirty little money secret. We have the largest endowment of any private school in the country, maybe even the world."

"Bigger than Harvard?" Willa asks.

"Bigger. Bigger than Princeton and Yale," Casey says. "Not to mention women's colleges like Smith."

You have arrived at the chapel door. You vaguely recognize several public figures mixed into the crowd. Proud faculty and alumni beam down at you as you pass the portal to the inside. It's your second time in the building, but the glistening carved wood of the magnificent Gothic Revival structure takes your breath away again. As your feet meet the immaculate floor, you feel a jolt of electricity, just like yesterday. You brush against Casey and exchange a little spark of static. It zaps her arm and she yanks it away, laughing.

You and your two friends find your assigned pew. You gaze around at the sea of plaid and navy and wave to Anupa who is two pews ahead. Seconds later the organ begins to play a triumphal march and two rows of Trumbull Woodhouse faculty and alums, who are called "Ancients," proceed down the aisle. As the organ music fades, the marching lines of women and a few men begin to chant. It sounds like one of the Gregorian chants you studied at Christmastime in music last year.

It is beautiful, haunting, and somber. Their deep voices fill up the air and end in a crescendo as the last marcher takes her place on the dais facing the assembled crowd. The singing stops and everyone is silent as a woman who looks old enough to be Yoda's wife appears from a narrow stone stairway behind the altar. She's wearing a cap, gown and stunning golden and embroidered sash, and she's carefully carrying a lit taper. You leaf through the Convocation Program that was waiting for you on your seat cushion and read that the light is lit from the "Eternal Flame of Wisdom." It's kept under lock and key in the Chapel Vault. Every year at Convocation, it is carried forward by the oldest living graduate, in the case Lauretia Jones, class of

1927. There is total silence as Mrs. Jones carefully lights eight tall pillar candles on either side of the Headmistress, Madame Cadwell, and the four deans.

As the Ancient raises her thin, frail arms, her right sleeve slips back to reveal a beautiful bracelet fashioned from aquamarine beads. It has several tattered, pink and yellow ribbons that look as old as she is. A gold lion's head charm dangles from the center bead.

"Oooh. Cool class bracelet," Willa breathes.

"We get class bracelets?" you whisper back. Something else you didn't know about Trumbull.

"Instead of rings. Every class designs their own. Fifth Form year. It's a top secret process. One of the few things my mom wouldn't tell me about going here," she adds.

You scan the well-manicured hands of the women sitting along the sides and front of the dais and notice many are wearing a bracelet on their right wrist. Each one is designed a bit differently. The women look on solemnly and respectfully as columns of pillar candles are being lit. Against a backdrop of ornate tapestries, steeply pitched gables, and imposing stone curtain walls, and amidst this bizarre ritual, they are the true royalty of Trumbull Woodhouse.

The chapel is silent as the prune-skinned, hunched-back woman replaces the special taper inside its glass case on the altar and locks the door. The key disappears under her robe and the ceremony continues.

"See the one with the cropped white hair and glasses? She's a retired Senator from New York. And that one on the end is the CEO of one of the TV networks. And the woman leaning over to Dean Acheson is the current President of the Ballentine Corporation. You know, the one famous for its billion dollar IPO last year?" Casey informs you in a nearly inaudible whisper. Casey's mom and grandmother went to Trumbull Woodhouse, and her father is on the board of trustees for the school, so she has dined and even danced with these regal women at cocktail parties and fundraisers since she was little. You can't imagine rubbing elbows with such powerful women. But at the Headmistress's luncheon later this afternoon, that's exactly what you'll be doing.

For now, you sit back and listen to Madame Cadwell deliver a stirring speech that sends shivers down your spine. She exudes a feeling of calm, steadiness and power. And you notice that as she speaks she takes time to make eye contact with nearly everyone.

"With great privilege comes great responsibility," she intones. Her eyes lock on yours. Was her timing intentional? You feel another electric surge and heat, like the other two you've felt here in the chapel yesterday and today. A rippling wave of relaxation and calm follows, and you breathe the smell of honeysuckle.

"If you listen to that little voice inside your head," Madame Cadwell continues, "I think you'll be surprised to find that you're actually not afraid of failing or being inadequate. Just the opposite. You're deepest fear is that the world will not recognize just how truly special and powerful you are. That little voice inside your head is telling you so. But how is anyone else supposed to get the message if you don't listen to it yourself?"

The tiny hairs on the back of your neck stand on end. It's as if she has read your thoughts, or at the very least the pages of your journal, and is speaking directly to you. "The author Marianne Williamson wrote about women that we ask ourselves, 'Who am I to be brilliant, gorgeous, talented, fabulous?' But I ask you today who are you not to be? She reminds you that playing small doesn't serve the world. There is nothing enlightened about shrinking so that other people won't feel insecure around you. For we are all meant to shine. Not just some of us…every single one of us. So as you begin your new year here at Trumbull Woodhouse, let your own light shine through. And give others the freedom, the respect, the encouragement to do the same. You are all sisters. Eternally bound by your experience here. And you will carry forth the Trumbull Woodhouse name and your soul's light into the world."

The Headmistress concludes her speech and steps down. For you, it was a call to action, and you can literally feel the meaning of her words as that little voice in your head stirs. A new sense of confidence and purpose is awakened in you and suddenly you want to live all four years of your life here at once.

Convocation wraps up with more stirring organ music. First the faculty, then the assembled Ancients, then assorted guests and finally you, the student body, from Sixth Form to Third Form file out. Everyone makes their way to Edith Cadwell's imposing four story colonial house perched on a rise overlooking the Great Lawn. It is bursting at the seams with three generations of Trumbull alumnae as you and your friends arrive.

You notice that the Ancients, who looked so monochromatic in the chapel, have each added a sash of color to their dark robes. Deep lilac, cotton candy pink, carrot orange, lemon yellow, periwinkle, crimson, harlequin green — each sash matches the color of the threading on the bracelets they all wear. They have lined up single file along Madame Cadwell's thick green lawn and perennial border, up the steps of her wraparound porch, and through the double screen entrance doors.

"I heard she has a duck pond in the back. I can't wait to see it!" Willa says, bending to see past your spot in line.

"I want to check out her reverse osmosis water system," Casey says adding a button to her lapel that reads "Recycling is a Religious Experience."

You shake hand after hand and smile into the glowing faces of younger graduates, women in their 20's and 30's who've successfully transplanted into the outside world. "It's a pleasure to meet you," you repeat over and over. And it is. It's a pleasure to imagine yourself standing there years from now with a budding career and a family of your own. It's a pleasure you want to chew on and savor until the last thought has been digested and then shake another hand for another bite. As you step into the house and through the maple-wood foyer, the line snakes into a living room where champagne colored drapes form rich pools of taffeta on the floor. Kitchen staff are ladling punch into flutes.

An older woman with apricot skin seizes your hand with painful force. "Ow!" you yelp, loud enough for Casey and Willa to glance over in your direction.

"Well hello," she says, not caring about your discomfort and continuing to hold onto your hand.

You try to ignore the fringe of uneasiness that's tickling your fingertips and toes. "Hello, it's a pleasure to meet you. I'm—"

"Oh, I know who you are," she says, her cake batter voice dripping all over your hand. You're close enough to see that the charm dangling from her burgundy bracelet is a little gold fox with onyx eyes. She squeezes so hard, you wince and look up into her eyes – they are burnt umber and fiery with hatred. You smile nervously and try to move on, but you swear you hear a deep growl rising from the back of her throat. Suddenly, Elizabeth Wilmington appears beside you. Just moments ago, you had glanced down the line and seen her at the end, some fifty feet away, a baluster of dignity under the vaulted ceilings in the chef's kitchen.

"May I have a word with you?" she says firmly to the fox, grasping her elbow and unclamping her hand from yours. The woman scowls at Elizabeth and reluctantly leaves the line. The two of them step to the side near the pink bowl of punch, and although you continue to shake hands, you watch them.

"It's just like you to stick your nose where it doesn't belong," the woman says ready for a fight.

"It's just like you to terrorize a child. Have you completely lost your senses? She has nothing to do with it." Elizabeth's voice is trying to stay low and discreet.

"She has just as much to do with it as you and I do." The woman hurls her words at Elizabeth like rocks over a cliff. She doesn't care about who hears them or what damage they do. Girls are starting to stare, their hands dropping to their sides. Several other Ancients in the receiving line look nervously at each other. Out of the corner of your eye, you notice Chloe LaFleur, that strange French girl, practically in tears and staring fiercely.

"You are out of control, Victoria. You betrayed us, and you're lucky you're even allowed to step foot on this sacred ground. Don't push it by preying on the innocent just because power is slipping from your grasp!" Elizabeth roars, blowing Victoria's hair back with the gust of air that carries her words.

"Fuck you, Elizabeth," she snarls, her teeth glinting like fangs in the reflection on the silver tureens. "Everyone is just waiting for you to die." A gasp spreads through the crowd. Now everyone is watching.

"I've always known you were weak, but I didn't know you were this pathetic," Elizabeth says softly, her anger white hot in her dark eyes.

Victoria grabs a glass of punch and flings it in Elizabeth's face. The pink liquid splashes in her eyes and drips down her hot cheeks. Everyone in the room lets out a yelp and the walls suck up the air.

Victoria turns on her heels and storms out. You go from shocked to stunned when several women from the receiving line fall in behind her. If they ever look back or slow their swift gait, it is not until they are well out of sight, past the blueberry border at the edge of the property. Elizabeth accepts a napkin from Madame Cadwell, who rushed over when it was already too late, and pats her face and neck as she returns to her place.

She is now the anchor of the line. She reaches out to grasp your hand.

Back in your dorm after lunch, no one can stop talking about the scene at Madame Cadwell's. Anupa has joined you, Casey and Willa in your suite's living room. Even Hayden leaves her door open a crack so she can hear what you have to say.

"Okay, I don't know what freaks me out more," Willa says, pacing around the room, her hands waving in excitement. "That she threw a glass of punch in Professor Wilmington's face or threw the F-bomb!"

"I can't imagine what would make her flip out on you like that for no reason," Casey says.

"All I did was shake her hand, just like everyone else!" you reply. "I was looking at her bracelet...You know, one of those class bracelets everyone had on? Hers had a burgundy ribbon and a golden fox charm with black eyes. She started crushing my hand and when I looked up, her eyes were as dark as the fox's. It was like she was possessed or something."

Anupa, who never goes anywhere without her trusty laptop, has been typing away furiously. "Burgundy ribbon with a fox head charm, that bracelet belongs to Class of '61," she announces.

"Where'd you find that?" Casey wants to know.

"Someone has created an anonymous forum on The Field. Everyone is commenting on what happened," Anupa says.

"When did Elizabeth Wilmington graduate? Maybe they're rivals?" Willa suggests as she pounces on Anupa and her laptop.

"I think I saw a yearbook from 1963 on her coffee table," you answer. "So they would have overlapped."

"Looks like they did a lot more than overlap," Casey says wryly.

Anupa's fingers scurry over the keys. "Bingo. Elizabeth Wilmington, formerly Elizabeth Gardner. Class of 1963. That's from the Ancients' page on the official school site," she adds.

"So who's Victoria in the class of 1961?" you ask.

"There is no Victoria that I can see. Maybe it's her middle name or a nickname? There are three women with V as a middle initial," Anupa reports staring hard at her screen. "But none with a photo."

Casey's competitive nature gets the best of her. She slips out of the room and return seconds later with her Macbook already fired up. She flops onto the sofa and logs into the same anonymous forum on The Field that Anupa is looking at.

"The creepiest thing was the way she said 'Hello,'" you continue. "She sounded like Count Dracula in search of fresh blood. And then, before I even said my name, she knew who I was! And that was when Elizabeth appeared."

"Whoa," Casey shrieks as her eyes rapidly scan her computer screen. "You guys are not going to believe this. Someone on the forum just wrote '...it has to do with Mount Demetria. And why no one is allowed to go there. Ask about the missing girls.'"

"What missing girls?" the three of you say in unison.

Casey glances nervously at the closed door to your suite to make sure it's safe and leans forward.

"I'm not supposed to know about this," she begins. "But my dad is on the Board of Trustees and I once overheard my parents talking about it."

Everyone moves a few inches closer. Willa's eyes sparkle with anticipation, and Anupa has actually stopped typing and closed the cover on her laptop.

"About 25 years ago, three Fifth Form girls went back into the area leading to Mount Demetria. Apparently it was always off limits to students and they were doing it on a dare from a bunch of Sixth Formers. They disappeared for three whole days. The school hired over 400 people to search the area, but they couldn't find a trace of any of them. Then, in the middle of the night on the third day, they walked down off the mountain. Everyone rushed to their sides with blankets, food and water, but the girls refused. All they said was they needed to go to the chapel."

"Were they hurt?" you croak in horror.

"Nope. Not a scratch, Well, except for two things. After they reached the chapel, they were catatonic, and they couldn't...or wouldn't...close their eyes. Not even for a second to blink. People said that something they saw scared them so deeply, they wouldn't shut their eyes ever again. And they had to be institutionalized. The rumor is that the school still pays for their care to this day," Casey finishes, glancing at the closed door one more time.

"Now that is a good story," Anupa grins, raising her hand for a high five.

Hayden's door suddenly swings wide open. "I don't know about any of you, but I plan on actually doing well this semester, which means I need to study," she announces. "Why don't you take your little nerdfest elsewhere?" Then she slams her door.

The four of you stare bug-eyed. A wadded up ball of paper bounces off her door. You glance back and see Willa grinning with pride over hitting her target. But Anupa rises to her feet.

"She's right – I mean, about the work stuff. I should get going," she apologizes hastily. "I have other work to do too."

Casey looks at her watch. "I suppose we all need to crack the books." She reluctantly stands up. Even Willa goes along. "I think I'll dig into the first assignment for Women In Sacred Texts. How about you?" she asks, turning your way.

"I was thinking maybe Biology," you say with a nervous smile. It's the exaggerated one you flash whenever you're trying to keep from panicking. Right now your stomach feels queasy.

Start studying? Already?

Here you were thinking you'd all spend Sunday afternoon – your last free afternoon for months – baking chocolate chip cookies or painting your nails on toes splayed with toilet paper dividers. Even playing Gin Rummy for potato chip currency in the common room.

Instead, the only sound is the lonely, muffled chirp of a cricket that snuck into the dorm three days ago when the movers in brown jumpsuits left the door propped open to carry in ridiculously opulent furnishings.

You want to cry out. It's your last night of carefree freedom, right? Wrong!

"Just getting a head start," Casey sighs as she pulls out Camus' The Stranger for her French class. The stuffed ravioli you had at the luncheon suddenly hardens like a stone and sinks to the bottom of your stomach. You tiptoe to your room and close the door behind you, suddenly feeling the suffocating weight of the Sunday Blues. You let yourself sink to the floor and stare at your desk. It's piled high with textbooks and first day assignments. Your heart begins to beat too fast and your pulse crashes in your skull. What if I can't do this? What if I'm not smart enough? You worry. These other girls don't even have the pressure of keeping a B average and they're already buckling down with the books.

You let the tears leak from your eyes. After a few minutes, you try to calm yourself down – breathing in through your nose and out through your mouth like Emily's mom taught you. It helps a little. You pull yourself up and sift through the papers for your schedule. Maybe if you can just take it one day at a time, it won't seem so impossible. Biology, Pre-Calculus, Ancient Greek. Greek? Are they kidding? It was that or Latin, a two year requirement for one or the other. Some girl in line at the Nest informed you that you have one of the hardest professors in the entire school – Gwendolyn Winterbourne – when you bought your term books.

You have to stay calm. Crying yourself to sleep is not an option. Neither is throwing yourself out the window. After all, it's only two floors up. You glance at the packet of Greek conjugations. It looks like alien hieroglyphics. Slow, deep breaths, you tell yourself, and put it back in the pile.

You crack open your biology textbook. Little white veins spread down the new spine as it's bent for the first time. You prop yourself up on your bed and begin to read about cellular respiration.

Meanwhile, every cell in your body is remembering to breathe.

The first three days of classes are a complete and total blur. For the first time you know what those little hamsters feel like running inside their plastic barrels. You step onto your wheel at 7:00 each morning, and the hours spin out from beneath you so fast you can barely stay standing. Then you go and go until you collapse in your bed at 10:00 PM. No time for making lists and really no need. Your schedule is packed so tight, there's no room. Your eyes are ready to close before your head hits the pillow.

Gordon Mitchell finally catches up with you between athletics and dinner on Wednesday.

"How's it going?" he asks, with a voice as soothing as a glass of warm milk.

Help me! you want to shriek. You want to throw yourself to the ground and cling to his knees. I'm overworked, sleep deprived, and scared out of my mind of flunking out!

All you say is, "I'm a little tired. I think I'll get used to it."

He purses his lips to show he understands and gives you a comforting smile. "Hang in there. The first month is always the worst."

First month? At this rate, you don't know how you're going to make it past the first week.

Public school began last week in Hatterly. You could be there, you think, ambling down the loaf brown linoleum hallways, goofing around with Emily. Granted, instead of honeysuckle and sandalwood, you'd be breathing in the stale sandwiches and sweaty gym shoes seeping from the grimy lockers, but at least you wouldn't be having anxiety attacks about grades churning up ulcers in your stomach. The most demanding thing on the schedule at Hatterly High, you think, is cross-country training.

You've always been smart and done well in school. It's the one thing you actually had control over. And whether you read for a grade or enjoyment, books have provided the easiest escape from your less-than-fabulous life. You didn't ever mind studying math or science and you always had a special love for the stories you learned in English and history. You spent your days with your nose buried in book. Making straight A's never took much effort. Until now.

You cannot believe the amount of work they assign and expect you to complete each night. What's worse is that some girls, like Hayden and Casey, don't seem to have to study as much as you do. And they certainly don't seem stressed about it.

Hayden spends more time on body exfoliation and perfecting her smoky eye make-up than her math homework. And Casey has managed to find time in her schedule to work with the Kitchen staff to begin a composting program. You almost faint when she tells you her plans to launch the French language version of *"La Vie en Vert"* (aka, The Green Life) next month. She has also landed a spot on the JV soccer team, hugging you sympathetically and patting your back like a mom burping her baby when she heard you only made first string intramural. If she weren't one of your best friends, you'd want to strangle her in her sleep.

Of all your classes, including Ancient Greek with the infamous Winterbourne, one of your biggest sources of difficulty is Pre-Calculus. Your teacher, Professor Peirce, is a doughy, disagreeable man who smells of stale cigars and combs his last few wisps of hair over the crown of his head. He manages to stare down at you even though he teaches from his fancy leather club chair, with his arm crooked behind his neck, and his polka dot bowtie tied to his thick neck like a leftover Christmas present. You are petrified of him calling on you, but of course he already has three times. He makes every girl stand when called on and makes you start your answer over if you say "like" or "um" or don't stand up straight.

The one bright, shining spot in the hour of math misery is Anupa. The two of you clicked right from the start, and the more you are around her, the more you like her. You feel more comfortable with her, despite your wildly different backgrounds, than anyone else at school. Even Casey. She's not really into primping, or working out, or gossip. The only make-up she wears is a custom pigment powder she orders from an art supply store in Canada, which she dabs on as eye shadow. It makes her look exotic, like one of the multi-armed, multi-colored deities depicted on the tapestry hanging over her bed.

In addition to saving your butt in Pre-Calculus about six times in four days, she's off the charts brilliant when it comes to programming, web design, Internet tools, and anything techie. Sometimes you forget she is your age.

You are sitting together in chapel during Friday morning Assembly when Dean Acheson lets a few bombs drop. In addition to the usual announcements – Model U.N. is meeting Sunday afternoon, a Jane Austen film festival kicks off this weekend – she mentions that two girls have withdrawn.

"I regret to announce that Andrea Hess and Olivia Knight, both Third Formers, have had to withdraw for personal family reasons. We send them best wishes as they go on their way," she states. A roar of whispers begins to rise.

"Girls, please, attention. On a lighter note, Trumbull Woodhouse will be hosting an Open Library for Newland School this Sunday from 1 till 5:00 PM," she continues. This time she smiles at the whoops and cheers.

You and Anupa exchange a confused look. You lean forward and tap Casey, in the pew directly ahead of you, for an explanation. She glances back. Her smile faintly twitches as her eyes meet Anupa's but then reforms into a bowed arch when she sees you. You're not sure why, but they both seem to rub each other the wrong way.

"Open Library means Newland School students can come over and use our library for the afternoon, because it's about ten times bigger and better than theirs. So this place will be crawling with guys," she explains, licking her lips. "For four whole hours! It's going to be so fun." This is the first time you've seen her get this excited over anything besides the new recycling bins in the student center.

A few rows past Casey, you can see Hayden and her posse., Their heads are bowed and clumped together. They are in deep discussion, probably about how to wear their hair or which push-up bra to use.

"It won't be fun for me," you say with a sigh. "I'll be banging out my Greek translation. That's if I'm not banging my head on the wall. I'll be lucky if I even have time to eat."

Anupa, who's not having a much easier time in Latin, nods sympathetically.

"And there's one more announcement of particular importance. Kirsten Ross has lost a piece of jewelry with unusual sentimental value. Kirsten?" Dean Acheson gestures. "I want you all to give her your undivided attention."

A pretty-ish girl with strawberry blonde hair climbs the stairs of the dais and speaks in a haltering voice.

"It's a necklace, by Cathy Waterman, made up of tiny gold and diamond daisies," Kirsten explains. "It's very delicate and small. I misplaced it on Wednesday. I normally wear it all the time, but I took it off for Field Hockey. My grandmother gave it to me last year just before she passed. If anyone finds it, please just bring it to my room in Moser Hall, or leave it at the Administration Offices."

"Thank you Kirsten," Dean Acheson says. "Assembly dismissed."

The throng of girls surges out of the Chapel doors riding a wave of chatter. You overhear several girls talking about the withdrawals.

"Andrea Hess had a good reason to leave. Her mom was just diagnosed with breast cancer. But Olivia Knight just went totally bonkers. She couldn't take the pressure."

So it's not only you, you think wistfully.

"I heard they had to carry her to the car," someone else adds.

Anupa shakes your arm and repeats what she just said.

"Hey, do you think someone may have stolen that girl's necklace?" Anupa whispers out of the side of her mouth.

"I doubt it," you reply. "Why would anyone here have to steal?" you wonder.

Most girls at TW had their own stockpiles of gold and diamonds in satin lined boxes and porcelain dishes in their rooms. No need to covet someone else's. But if someone did steal the necklace or want to keep it once found, the fractured detail about Kirsten's dead grandmother probably wouldn't have the effect she intended it to have. It wouldn't lodge in the thief's conscience like a sharp shard of guilt, festering and throbbing so painfully that she had no choice but to return the necklace for relief.

It would just pass through the gaping hole in her conscience that let her take what isn't hers in the first place, you think.

Finally, the weekend is here! I'm using my precious moments of rest and relaxation this Saturday morning to start a shimmer journal.

I just bought this at the Nest. I was thinking of keeping this on my laptop, but how could I pass up this amazing book of blank pages? It was just begging to be filled up. The cover is Robin's egg blue grosgrain ribbon, crisscrossed by narrow yellow satin. The pages are big, fresh, and startlingly white.

I need to figure these shimmers out. I want to understand them. This is probably something I should've done a long time ago. But I'm doing it now. I have to. They are coming more often since I arrived, and I need a place where I can write them down. I want to see if there is a pattern — any common images or triggers that I could use to start to control these things.

Stuff I plan to record for every shimmer:

1. Detailed description: every thing I see, smell, feel and sense during the vision; any stray thoughts that come to me while it's going on.

2. Date, Time and Conditions under which the shimmer arrived.

Cadwell's Convocation speech, corny as it sounds, made me realize I should look at these things as something special. That I'm special.

There has to be a bigger meaning, a reason for getting them because not everyone does. I've always asked 'Why me?' and felt sorry for myself, like this is some cruel curse. But maybe I should be asking 'Why me?' looking for a greater purpose. What is the purpose of these mental movies?

3. Follow up notes: what happens afterward. Does the shimmer help me or hurt me? Is it my early warning system?

Shimmers this week:

Tuesday, I was already in the shower, when the wake-up bell rang. I saw my name being written in that old crumbling book again. Women were chanting in the background. This is the first time that I have had the same shimmer twice. I still can't see what else is being written. But I know it is about me. It was around 7 AM and probably lasted a couple of minutes. Afterward, while I was getting dressed in my room, I felt like everything around me was heightened somehow. Like the volume of planet earth had been turned up. I could feel every fiber of my clothing and smell everything, even dust. My body felt electric, like sparks could fly off of it any minute.

During the day, I could hear the echo of a bird flapping its wings as it flew from one tree to the next. But I felt exhilarated rather than scared. By evening, these symptoms had worn off.

Follow-up: nothing so far.

With only 170 pages to read for Women in Sacred Texts, and a single problem set for Pre-Calculus, Saturday felt almost like a mini-vacation. But today is Sunday, and it's a different story.

Your first major assignment is due tomorrow: Gwendolyn Winterbourne's notorious two-page Ancient Greek translation for first year students. Winterbourne – Winnie to the survivors of her first year – is infamous for using this first assignment to weed out the Greek goddesses from the mere mortals. After a mind-numbing first week of trying to learn the crazy alphabet and a less than stellar performance in a grammar parsing competition, you don't think you'll have to worry about falling from any pedestals. You're just hoping to keep your place in the class of 20__.

During your little tour, Regan warned you that the professors here usually form their opinion of you in the first couple weeks. And it sticks.

So you wake up early, grab some tea and toast from the nearly empty dining hall, and get to work. Letter by letter, word by word, sentence by sentence, you begin to transform the pages into intelligible paragraphs of modern English. You work steadily, until your butt goes numb in the chair. You get up and pace around your room to let the blood flow again and then dutifully return to your post. Through the open windows, you can hear snippets of conversations and spurts of laughter as people walk by outside.

You wish you could be outside in the sunshine or even curled up in the common room, but you know better. Casey sticks her head in to invite you to lunch, but you decline. You've worked your plan and planned your work, and you're going to finish this if it kills you.

By 3:00 in the afternoon, you are almost done – except for four phrases that you cannot find in any of the three Greek dictionaries you have bought or borrowed. Now what? You wander outside your room for the first time since breakfast, but Rose House is a ghost town. Lily Mitchell is downstairs bringing some groceries in, and you decide to ask her advice.

"Oh, there's a wonderful rare book division of the library here, called The Porter Collection. They have some very rare dictionaries of Greek from 17th and 18th century England. Try them!" she offers encouragingly. "And they're open on Sunday afternoons. Don't forget to sign in at the main desk."

"Great," you reply, turning to head out the door.

Lily tilts her head to the side and squints her eyes. "Are you sure you don't want to change first?" You look down. So maybe you won't be at the top of anyone's Best Dressed List sporting Soffe shorts, an old gray sweatshirt, and flip flops, but it's Sunday, people. And this thing is due in three hours.

"Breathing is a luxury at this point, forget fashion," you say as you head towards the front door.

Lily just laughs. "Okay, then. Good luck."

You've noticed the sign for The Porter Collection a few times in the past week, but you had no idea what it was. The library is surprisingly busy.

Oh great. Newland is here.

There are so many guys and girls milling around outside, it looks like a rock concert. That would explain how empty the rest of campus is. A flush of shame burns your cheeks and spreads down your neck. Now you wish you had put a little more thought into your outfit, or at least shampooed. As you walk through the main reading room, a few girls stare over their books and down their noses at you. A couple of them point and whisper to their friends who whip around in their club chairs to get a look for themselves. But you plow through. You knew you would turn a few heads with your bedhead look, but this is ridiculous.

"Excuse me, I need an Ancient Greek dictionary, one from The Porter Collection?" you ask at the desk.

"Straight up the stairs, the first door on your right," the woman behind the desk answers crisply without removing her eyes from her reading.

You climb the stairs two by two, and at the top, a middle-aged man in a pale blue sweater directs you to the stacks. Row 11, Shelf 23. But when you get there, instead of a leather-bound answer to your prayers, there is nothing but a gaping hole and a column of dust. You place your hand where the dictionary is supposed to be and hang your head in defeat.

"Just my luck," you mumble falling against the row of books. "I give up. You win Winterbourne," you call out as you clutch the shelf in desperation.

"Aw, c'mon. It can't be that bad," you hear a deep voice say from behind you.

You spin around and see a vaguely familiar face. Green eyes. Shaggy brown hair.

"You're right. It's not that bad, it's worse," you reply dryly. Then it hits you. "Hey, aren't you that guy from the airplane in South Carolina?"

"Yeah! You remembered," he retorts happily. "Austin Burlingame," he adds jutting out his hand. You shake and introduce yourself.

"How could I forget? You were practically sitting on my lap."

He winces but his head bobs up and down in agreement. "My mom used to say I was like a bull in a china shop. She put rubber bumpers on the corners of the countertops when I was little."

"And I thought I was a handful," you tease.

"How's your finger?"

You hold up your pinky. "Still there."

"Nice. I saw you come into the library and was like 'no way! I know that girl.' So I decided to come say hi," he explains, his arms and hands gesturing nervously.

"Well, I'm glad you did." And you are. Austin has a sweetness about him that makes him easy to talk to. Instead of getting all nervous and saying the wrong thing, you feel completely relaxed around him. It's a nice change.

"You are?" he whispers, his eyes big and green like the Great Lawn. He catches himself and clears his throat loudly. "Is it hot in here?" he asks suddenly tugging at the collar of his button down.

"Don't ask me. I'm due for a meltdown. They seem to come once a week these days," you say slipping your hands in your back pockets glancing around.

"I know! Me too. If my Spanish class doesn't kill me, my human genome presentation will. Or there's always my Dad if I don't make good grades."

"For me it's Greek," you say, motioning to the shelf.

"Oh yeah? My roommate's brother is an upperclassman. I heard him say that old dude in the blue sweater is like a Greek genius."

"Really?" you say scrunching your nose in disbelief. "Good to know, thanks."

"Are you looking for this?" a girl's voice asks. "The Wharton Dictionary?" You both turn this time and see a pale girl with glasses standing in the aisle. You recognize her from Greek class. She sits in the last seat in the last row and always chews on the ends of her sepia brown hair. She dumps the old leather volume into your hand and walks away.

"Careful what you wish for, you just may get it," you say sarcastically holding up the book. "Time to go Greek," you say rolling your eyes.

"Yeah, I gotta get back too. Hey, do you like The Snowcones?" he blurts out.

"The what?" you ask.

"The Snowcones. They're an indie pop band. They recorded their first single when they were our age. How about the Mighty Mud Bugs? The Jackpots? They just signed with Rightside Records. The Crash? They're my favorite," he says firing off band names and factoids.

"No, I'm sorry. I don't," you say shaking your head, amazed by his energy.

"Oh, man, you're missing out. Okay, I'm gonna burn some stuff for you. It's going to open up a whole new world. Wait till you hear 'Worse for the Where,' by the Crash. It'll change your life."

"Okay," you laugh. "See you around, Austin."

"See you," he says staring after you as you turn and slip out of the stacks. After a few minutes of scanning the stacks, you spot the alleged Greek guru on an early dinner break. His name is Gary Beckett and Austin was right, he knows more about the language of the Gods than Zeus himself. Gary gives you just the right clues to help crack the code of your last paragraph of translation. And he even offers to re-shelve the Wharton Dictionary for you.

"Thank you, Gary. I owe you one," you say gratefully.

"Nonsense. You owe me nothing except your lifelong dedication to studying ancient Greek and naming your firstborn Gary, even if it's a girl," he teases.

You laugh and wave goodbye as you start off for the stairs. You are beginning to feel relief course through your veins. But when you glance up at the big round clock hanging over the landing, you do a double take. You only have twenty-six minutes before the paper is due and you still have to get back to your dorm and type everything up.

You dart down the steps and sprint through the library to the big wooden doors. As you heave one open, the most beautiful boy you've ever seen is standing in your path. His peacock blue eyes lock with yours and you swear you hear angels sing. You must look like a deer in headlights. Stunning, heavenly blue headlights that you hope never turn away. Your hand goes limp and you drop your notes. He bends to pick them up.

"Here you go," he says with a movie-star smile. His voice sends bolts of electricity straight to your heart. You grip the paper with both hands, almost tearing it in half, to keep from reaching out and touching him like a lovesick fan.

"Hey Connor, come on," you hear a guy call out from behind

you. You glance back and see another older boy standing in the library lobby with two Sixth Formers, each prettier than the next. You can feel yourself turning red down to the roots of your hair.

"Thanks. Excuse me," you mumble as you brush past.

You steal one last glance at his painfully perfect face and hurry outside. Little pieces of your heart break off and fall on the floor all around him. You'll have to look up this Greek God online later. It can be your reward for turning in your translation.

When you get back with your notes from the library, Hayden is perched on the couch in your suite's common room holding court with her handmaidens Erica and Danielle. With perfect hair, polished nails, and killer clothes, they look like a photo shoot for Teen Vogue. They gasp and cover their mouths in horror and amusement when they see you.

"So the rumor is true," Hayden says, looking you up and down with lightly disguised delight.

"What are you talking about?" you ask, trying to sound nonchalant. It's the first time she's talked to you in almost a week.

"You actually wore your pajamas to the library visitation with Newland," Hayden drawls. Erica and Danielle laugh maniacally in unison as if she just delivered the punch line to the funniest joke ever told.

"Hayden, what you don't get is that the person under the clothes matters more than the clothes themselves," you fire back, surprised by your own eloquence.

All three of their heads cock back in indignation. Her lips curl. "That's just what poor people say who can't afford good clothes," Hayden snaps, her words as sharp as her freshly painted fingernails.

You roll your eyes and cross to your room without a response. There's more tittering as you shut your bedroom door, but you ignore it. Her words can't hurt you. Not today.

You push thoughts of Hayden out of your head and focus on the last bit of translation. With the miraculous help from Gary Beckett and with five minutes to spare, you finally send in your Greek translation to Blackboard, Trumbull Woodhouse's portal website for submitting class assignments. Each section of each class has its own virtual bulletin board. The Blackboard tracks the date, the time and the identity of the person submitting. There is no way to fudge a late paper and no chance to proffer excuses. It's quick and confidential. "And it saves paper," Casey always reminds you.

A little green check mark flashes on your screen – Successfully Sent! Exactly eleven hours and fourteen minutes after you started, your monstrous Ancient Greek assignment is finished. You are famished and head straight to the Snack Shack (throwing on a black sweater, a little makeup, and changing shoes first) where you order a grilled cheese with tomato and a vanilla shake.

You're still not sure how you did, but you tried your best. That used to count for something. And you saw that gorgeous boy as a bonus.

An hour later, you are propped up on pillows on the floor of Casey's room, staring at the flawless face of Connor Blackman on your laptop screen.

"Everyone Google stalks and does Field checks these days," Casey says shrugging off your embarrassment as you both eagerly await his picture to complete.

"Oh my God, he's gorgeous!" she squeals, grabbing the screen and wrenching it towards her.

"Hey, easy on the laptop," you cry, protecting your first love from her Vulcan death grip.

"That's the guy you met at the library?" she says in amazement. "How come I don't meet guys like that?" she huffs.

"I guess it was just meant to be," you say wistfully, clutching your heart and staring up at the ceiling in rapture.

She elbows you and clicks through his profile on The Field. "This is all PG rated stuff. You know who you should ask to get the real scoop on this guy? Willa's brother," she says.

Everett Nash is a Fifth Former at Newland, and according to Casey "super cool" and "really hot." She and Willa spent the afternoon hanging out with him at the library this afternoon.

"Good idea," you reply. You stare at his image for a few more second. "Hey! Should I invite him to be my friend?" you say daringly. Your heart races just at the thought of it.

"Sure, you and 141 other of his nearest and dearest female fans. This guy is a collector," she says disdainfully.

"It's just The Field. It's not like a marriage proposal. Who couldn't use another friend?" you say, trying to sound innocent.

"*Use* being the operative word in his case," she says skeptically.

"What do you mean 'use'?" you bristle. Would Casey give you bad advice out of jealousy? you wonder.

"An older guy who looks like that, with 140 other girls as friends... I don't know. Just be careful."

You glance down at the little flashing icon next to Connor's name. Your heart is beating so fast, you actually feel light-headed. With one click of the mouse, you could be his friend. Or you could be totally humiliated. One of the two. Your palms are moist with sweat but your throat is dry. That figures. Your body is going haywire. You close your eyes.

Click.

You have chosen to invite CB@Newland to be your friend.

"No!" Casey wails. But it is too late.

Just as a twinge of regret pricks your heart, the hot pink bubble indicating a new IM from The Field pops up on your desktop.

CB@Newland accepts your invitation.

You let out a shriek of delight and Casey rolls her eyes.

"Just make sure you talk to Everett," she says.

You are exhausted, but you find it hard to fall asleep. You wake up the next morning still thinking about the translation. You know you should just forget about it until the grade comes back. There's really no sense in agonizing over whether you made mistakes now that it's finished.

Professor Winterbourne doesn't say a word about your papers when you get into class on Monday, which drives you crazy. She just sits there, her long, wrinkly neck poking out of her ruffle collar like an old turkey wearing a doily. She makes a clucking noise from her throat about every fifth word. She announces that class will end a few minutes early so her teaching assistant can schedule times to go over your translations in the next week. But she asks you to stay. You smell a sulfurous odor of trouble as you remain in your seat. You dig your nails into the palm of your hand to focus on something other than the twelve pairs of eyes nervously glancing your way. Some of your classmates look more frightened than you are. You face feels hot. You must look like a lobster. You are certainly in the hot seat.

"I did not receive your paper," Professor Winterbourne informs you as the last of the students has filed out. Her voice is chilly and critical. The skin on her neck vibrates as she speaks.

"That's impossible!" you cry. "I sent it last night from my dorm room. "To the Blackboard. It was exactly on time."

She warbles on, ignoring your protest.

"You may expect some kind of special treatment, due to your personal circumstances, but Trumbull Woodhouse is not that kind of school, and I am certainly not that kind of professor. No student in my class is more special than the rest."

Her neck skin is doing a full-on jiggle that belies her calm tone.

"I don't expect any special treatment, Professor Winterbourne, at all. Ever. You have to believe me, I turned my paper in. I got the little green check mark and everything."

And you did! This can't be happening.

"I will have to take off half of a letter grade for tardiness, and 15 demerits," she continues, "but if you have the assignment in to me by the end of the academic day, I will accept it. Just this once. No one is perfect, but I give only one free pass. So I hope you've used yours wisely," she clucks and dismisses you abruptly.

"Yes, Professor," you reply meekly. You can feel tears building in the backs of your eyes so you quickly leave her classroom before they start to flow. As you reach the hallway, someone leaves the classroom opposite and you glance up. Of course it has to be Samantha Carden, the coolest and most popular teacher in the school. She looks meaningfully in the direction of Winterbourne and rolls her eyes, as if to say "don't let her get to you." Then she gives you a big smile before walking away.

You are so stunned by her friendly gesture, you actually do

begin to cry. Your thoughts get all soggy when you do, which has never served you well. You need to figure out what happened to your paper, so your brain can't be soaking in a pool of saltwater tears. You quickly drag the sleeve of your cardigan across your eyes and hurry down the hall just as the warning bell rings for next period.

You rush from your own personal Greek tragedy to a fate worse than death – Pre-Calculus. Just as the final bell rings, you bolt into the classroom and speed to your seat like that cartoon roadrunner. Your cheeks have gone from a humiliated hue of red to a flushed pink, as you had to sprint the entire way there. Well, almost the entire way. Except for the minutes you were shimmering! The last thing you need is to be late to Peirce's class and have more demerits rain down on you so soon after Winterbourne's wrath.

How could this have happened? It doesn't make sense! I sent that paper in, maybe there was there a problem with the server? But I got the confirmation! I'm certain.

You are so preoccupied with your missing Greek paper that you don't hear Professor Peirce's harsh voice calling out your name. Anupa elbows you in the ribs to warn you. You blink several times, trying to clear the chatter from your head. Isabel

Ortega is returning to her seat after writing the equation from problem number 74 in the workbook on the board. It's your turn to get out of your chair, go up to the board and solve it.

These seem like simple functions. Even a robot could do them. But your brain is not working correctly. Your legs feel like bowls of Jello, and you keep replaying the movie of submitting your assignment over and over again in your head. The chalky white numbers and symbols fade and blur into a white haze.

Professor Peirce gets annoyed, actually rising from his puffy leather chair for the first time all year. The class leans back in their seats. He could blow at any minute! He says your name one, last, gruff time, but you don't react fast enough. Anupa jumps out of her chair, races to the blackboard, and scribbles the solution to the equation before Peirce finishes your name! Peirce just stares back at her for a moment, stunned by what just occurred. His mouth open and closes like a little fish out of his tank.

Anupa shrugs her slender shoulders and tips her head to the side. "Sorry, Professor Peirce. I just love polynomials so much, I couldn't help myself," she says, her words pouring out like sweet cream.

He can't really fault her for loving math so much or solving the equation. And her answer was exactly right, by the way. But no one has ever gone out of turn in his class. No one has dared. His parched lips pucker into a disapproving puss. But he lets it go.

"Sit down, Miss Lahiri," he says sharply. "Please refrain from going out of turn or I'll be forced to give you demerits. If you love equations that much, you won't mind doing one through thirty-two from the Extra Help section in the back of the workbook. Have them done by next class."

Anupa nods cheerfully, as if this is a privilege. She skips back to her seat next to you. With her back to Peirce, her face drops and she sticks out her tongue. You mouth the words "I'm sorry" and "thank you" as she sits down. As the remaining minutes drag by, you keep one ear on the lesson but the rest of your awareness is on that paper. The bell rings, and you jump up, pulling Anupa aside.

"I'm so sorry! I owe you big time!" you say thankfully.

"Don't worry about it. I can do those equations in my sleep," she says flapping her hand down in dismissal. And she can, that's the best and worst part. "Why were you so spaced today?" she asks, adjusting the strap on her backpack.

"My Greek assignment never posted! The big translation, the one I worked on for twelve hours yesterday," you wail.

You suddenly realize Anupa is the exact person you need. You were so freaked out, you hadn't thought of it before. But who better to help solve this technological catastrophe than Miss MySpace herself?

"What do you mean? It never posted?!" Anupa's interest is sparked.

You walk with her to lunch, explaining everything that happened on the way. You both make peanut butter and jelly sandwiches in the dining hall, and head back to your dorm room to check out your Blackboard account. The sooner you resend your translation to Winterbourne, the better. You want her to know you really do have it, ready and waiting on your hard drive and that you weren't just trying to buy time to finish it.

You toss your backpack on the bed without looking and balance yourself anxiously on the edge of your desk chair. As you wait for your laptop to fire up and load Blackboard, Anupa plops onto your bed. A pink marabou feather swirls up in front of her and slowly drifts back down to the floor.

"Have you been dying chickens pink and sacrificing them in here again?" she jokes taking a big bite of her sandwich.

"Believe me, I would if it would make the grade gods happy," you say snidely. "Looks like a feather from one of Hayden's frou-frou slippers."

"The Queen of Mean was in your room?" Anupa inquires through a sticky mouthful of bread and peanut butter. She almost chokes at the thought.

"I doubt it. She was complaining the other day about some feathers falling off."

"But how did it get all the way in here?" Anupa asks skeptically.

But before you can answer, the Blackboard website pops up, and you make two shocking discoveries.

"My Blackboard account is empty," you gasp. You and Anupa go through every folder you've created, every message you've composed, and every file you've sent from your mail program since you got your computer. But the email with the Greek translation attached is nowhere to be found. It's as if it never happened!

"Just resend it from your hard drive," Anupa suggests. "Once it's officially sent, again, we'll get to the bottom of what happened the first time," she says with assurance.

Thank God for Anupa.

You go to your desktop and click on the folder you created for Greek, and that's when you make the second discovery. "Oh my God."

YOUR ENTIRE TRANSLATION ASSIGNMENT HAS DISAPPEARED FROM YOUR HARDDRIVE.

"But...how is that possible?" you ask Anupa, tears brimming but not falling.

Anupa's face smoothes over with calm, sheer determination. She shoos you out of your desk chair so she can sit at the controls. Her long, thin fingers flit and peck with lightning speed at the keys like the sickbills of a hundred hummingbirds. After what seems like seven years, but is really seven minutes, the clattering stops, her fingers hovering over the keys. She sits still, staring at the computer.

"Huh," she says.

Huh? That's it? Your entire life hangs in the balance and all she can say is "huh"? You feel like you could implode when her fingers suddenly resume, darting and stabbing the keyboard as she extracts more information from the jumble of computer code in the little white dialog box, like the sugary pollen from a cornflower.

"I have good news and bad news," she says, her eyes still glued to the screen.

"Good news, please. I need some good news," you say. Your anxiety leaves you drained and wilted. You sit on your bed and wait for the verdict.

"The good news is I was able to recover your paper," Anupa announces. "I just sent it to Winterbourne on Blackboard, to my account, and to the printer in my room, just in case. So you're safe there."

Your mood changes in an instant. You jump for joy, you are so relieved! "Oh my God, thank you, Anupa!" you shout, throwing your arms around her shoulders, forgetting the drama, fear, and embarrassment that has built up over the course of the morning. You don't care about anything else right now as long as that assignment is in! She laughs and hugs you back. But your happiness is short lived, as usual.

"The bad news is, someone definitely hacked into your Blackboard account," she says grimly, pointing to a line of gibberish on the screen.

"But who?" you ask, stunned and scared again. Now this is

serious.

"I can't tell yet. The IP address is anonymous. You don't see those very often. Whoever it was went in and intercepted your paper before it ever reached Winterbourne's mailbox. And then, some time this morning, they went through the server and removed it from your computer. Very impressive," she says, as though her opponent is in front of her.

"First The Field, and now this," you say quietly. "Should I report it?"

You don't know what to do or how to feel. You've never been the target of something like this. What first seemed like a frustrating computer glitch has turned into full-on sabotage. Perhaps the same person who trashed your translation wanted to trash your social reputation too! But you don't know anyone well enough to have enemies. Hayden thinks you're a drip, but...

"I wondered about that invitation being hacked when you first told me about it but I didn't want to mention it. Have you told your advisor?"

"No, I haven't seen her since that outburst at the convocation lunch and I heard she had to go out of town."

"Next time you see her, you should probably say something, but give me a little time first. Until then, you can send anything that's due through my account. I've got it encrypted so that Bill Gates himself couldn't get to it," she says confidently. "I want to check on a few things. The Field invitation mishap will be hard to trace because it was so long ago and went over public wires. But I could talk to Bailey about it. He's got access to the school server's back up and a lot of the codes that I don't," she says distractedly as if she's talking more to herself than you.

Her brain is already thinking ten steps and one thousand computer commands ahead.

Shimmer Journal-

Date: Monday of the Winterbourne's legendary Greek Assignment

Time: on my way to Pre-Calculus after Ancient Greek.

I was running late after Prof. Winterbourne chewed me out for missing the assignment! Which I didn't, but I couldn't prove it on the spot. The bell for next period rang and my shimmer started.

Description: Samantha Carden is stretched out on a lounge chair on the porch of a weathered, shingled house. Her straw colored hair whips around in the ocean breeze but she doesn't bother clearing it from her face. She stares out at the seagulls stepping through the bubbling white froth of the breaking waves just yards from the porch steps. The wind carries the echo of a dog barking down the beach. And I could almost feel the damp, salty air on my skin. Then the image faded.

Follow Up: I had just seen Professor Carden in the hall outside Greek. Also, the shimmer began, like the one in the shower last Tuesday, when I heard a bell ring.

For the next two days, your life calms down. Maybe it all really does get easier, like Gordon Mitchell promised. The size of your workload is still huge, but you must be adjusting. When Professor Baldur assigned 90 pages of reading in French class on Tuesday, you thought it was on the short side.

Today is your first intramural soccer scrimmage against the Archer School, a private day school about forty minutes away. Coach Carlson was very clear that everyone must be at the shuttle at 3 PM sharp. You need to make it there, play, and make it back before dinner service ends. So your away-game bag is already packed and sitting by your door.

You aren't particularly nervous about the match. The intramural league is more about participation than competition, and you've heard Archer's bark is worse than it's bite. An afternoon of running, defending, and hopefully scoring is exactly what you need. You have put the recent online sabotage out of your mind as much as you can. Anupa reported this morning that she's still working on it. And you'd rather have your eye on the ball than your mind's eye on the shimmers you've been having this past week. They are coming more often, and they seem to come in real time — showing you the present in addition to the future.

You have flashes of your friends, your teachers, and other people you don't even really know at school. It wasn't a big deal to get a glimpse of Willa checking her mail at the campus post office, or see Casey practicing her history presentation in front of her mirror. But there are some things you don't want to see – private moments, and personal problems that are none of your business. Although Professor Peirce is not your favorite person, you take no pleasure in shimmering him playing with a robot collection alone in his cottage after dinner. You'd rather not know Coach Carlson peruses an online dating service in the library late at night.

But sometimes your shimmers are sweet, like when you saw Bailey falling in love with Anupa. He's had a crush on her since he first saw her standing at orientation in her magenta dress with her black hair tied back in two long braids.

Bailey knows magenta is merely a function of light, the result of mixing red and blue wavelengths or removing lime-green from white, but that day it became the color of first love. It knocked him off his feet, and by the time he got up, it made him want to walk up to her and say "Marry Me" instead of tell her his name. Now his mouth forms that orange slice smile whenever he looks at a picture of her he keeps by his bed. In the privacy of his room at his parent's house in Harrowgate, he practices asking her out in the mirror and dances with a pillow in case he ever works up the nerve to do it in person. Maybe your shimmers aren't such a curse if they allow you to catch a glimpse of moments like that. Ones that are awkwardly wonderful and embarrassingly big-hearted. Ones that allow you to see the heart and mind of people like Bailey Anderson.

You've written each vision down in your new shimmer book, and so far, two things stick out. Shimmers seem to be triggered when you hear bells ringing or jingling. And the number 11 sticks out in a lot of them. Either the date, or the time, or something you are looking at when it begins, like the time you shimmered after running into Bella Morrison with the number "11" on her soccer jersey. Or the day you slipped into a shimmer at the Snack Shack after Casey counted out 11 jellybeans for herself in front of you.

Once you went back and read your shimmer book, you realized you were about to answer number eleven on the school's questionnaire when you shimmered on the airplane about the red van crash.

Last night's vision made goosebumps crawl up your arms. You shimmered Chloe LaFleur, the strange French girl, sitting sprawled out on a blanket under a tree in the woods behind the school greenhouse. She was writing in the red leather book she always has with her, iPod earbuds in place and candy wrappers strewn all around her. This is her most common state. She only has a couple friends, and that's if you count the equally snooty girls who stop by to say "Bonjour" or "Ça va?" at the lunch table where she sits alone. The rumor mill reports that she sent her bodyguards home, but that didn't make her any easier to approach. She only speaks French outside of class, if she speaks at all. But even with those elite girls who speak French in their sleep, Chloe only converses for a few moments before she gets a distant look in her eye, like she's in a different place. And whoever she's talking to moves away without Chloe having to say a word.

The garden scene only lasts a second, but just as the shimmer is fading, Chloe's head pops up and snaps to the right. Her nose twitches as if she's detected a strange scent, and just for an instant, you feel like she knows you're there. It's a jangly feeling, like when you first know a sneeze is coming on, but before it gets any bigger, Ah-Choo! You let out a sneeze and you're back in your dorm. And the feeling is gone.

You stop by your mailbox just after lunch and there are two notes: one from Amy Phillips, Winterbourne's T.A., with the time slot for your translation review and the other from Coach Carlson. The handwritten note says the scrimmage has been cancelled due to a broken pipe flooding the soccer field at the Archer School. It will be rescheduled for next week, so the team is to meet on the Upper Field at 3:15 for a light practice and dribble drills instead. You are really bummed. It would've been cool to get off campus and see another school. After biology, your last class, you sulk back to your room and put on your practice uniform, tossing the note on the desk and leaving your duffel bag by the door to unpack later.

But when you get to the Upper Field at 3:15 on the dot, you go from dejected to distraught. The practice field is empty. Not a teammate in sight. Where are they? Shooting pains of panic explode in your chest and ricochet like angry bees in a jar. Something inside you, call it intuition, tells you to go to the shuttle. You fly to the parking lot behind the gymnasium where the buses line up. Just as you are rounding the corner, you see the intramural team bus, packed with your teammates, your coach, and all of their game gear, pulling away. You yell out and try to stop them but they turn out the drive and are gone.

You drop to the curb, the cold concrete unforgiving and rough. What the hell is going on? you think to yourself.

With Anupa on the case of your Greek translation mishap, you had allowed yourself to believe everything was going to be okay. But now you have written proof that someone is out to get you. Are they just carrying out pranks or are they playing for keeps?

"When did you get the note?" Casey asks for about the fifth time.

"Right after lunch," you answer.

Casey and Anupa are sitting on your bed, staring slack-jawed at the soccer note.

"Aren't you going to say, 'Don't worry!' or 'It's just someone's idea of a silly joke?'" you plead.

You look into their equivocating eyes, little worry lines running across their foreheads like cracks in a dropped plate. You are beginning to think coming to this school was a big, stupid mistake.

"Oh I'm sure this is nothing! Just a stunt or a mean prank!" Anupa says quickly and a little too forcefully.

"Yeah, I agree with Anupa." Casey's voice breaks at the end as if it refuses to complete the lie her mouth is telling. "This is clearly someone from your team just putting you on. I'm sure it's all in good fun," she says, looking to Anupa for confirmation. Anupa smiles weakly but nods aggressively.

Seeing the two of them sitting so close to each other, agreeing, working in tandem, gives you a warm prickly feeling that seems like comfort...or maybe it's dread. Your two best friends don't usually get along this well. It's not that they don't like each other. A competitive edge drives them apart and makes them jumpy and twitchy when you all hang out. They're both math whizzes, science geniuses, and love NPR, so you thought they'd hit it off. But Anupa incites Casey by playing devil's advocate on environmental issues and world politics. And Casey challenges Anupa on the ethics of her internet hacking.

Girls pay Anupa big bucks to read private files on the boys from Newland School or access the origins of the Dating Diary, an anonymous tell-all site about boys, sex, and scandals. Anupa always requires a good cause, no matter how much her customers are willing to shell out, but this still sends Casey's moral compass spinning. They both think the other is a show-off and have told you so on several occasions.

You can't decide if their alliance tonight is because they're just being good friends and putting their differences aside, or if the situation is so bad that it stirs their rivalry, each trying to out-help the other.

The next day, you show the note to Coach Carlson. She doesn't buy your story about missing the bus. "Why would I handwrite twenty-three notes to every girl on the team when I could print them out in two seconds, or send an email?" she asks. As if you were supposed to think of that even though the note is on official TW letterhead!

"Besides, that's nowhere close to my handwriting. I've written enough plays on the board, you should know that by now," she says unsympathetically. But when she sees you fighting back tears, she softens a little. "Look, it's not that I don't believe you. It's just that your absence nearly cost us the game. We had two girls go out in the first half, and we would've had to forfeit if Francesca hadn't played on her bad knee."

She ends up giving you forty demerits and a promise to punish anyone on the team who you can prove had something to do with the note. With the fifteen demerits from Winterbourne, you are up over the dreaded 50 mark. A penalty of some sort will have to be paid.

Right now all you want to do is get into bed, pull the covers over your head, and not come out for the rest of the trimester. You wish you weren't such a magnet for trouble. You wish your parents would've held onto you. You wish you didn't always have to take care of yourself.

And for an instant you wish you'd never come to this mystifying, beautiful school where the only thing more perfect than the campus are its inhabitants. You wish you didn't shimmer, or feel out of place, or unwanted.

But at this moment, most of all, you wish you didn't have to go to your meeting with Amy Phillips. She's a bright-eyed alum who is so desperate to be a TW teacher, she's willing to endure three trimesters as Winterbourne's assistant just to get on staff. If Winterbourne gives her a good report, she'll be considered for a permanent position in Classics next year. So Amy wakes up early to be the first one to arrive at the Classics department and stays late, well after the lights have been turned off and everyone else is gone. You've seen her in your shimmers, still there when the mice creep out from a little hole in the wall near the water cooler. She waits, just in case Winterbourne decides to come back. And she schedules evening meetings with students so she won't feel so lonely while she waits.

But your meeting actually goes well. She sits down to review her marks, but there weren't many on your paper. You got a B+, and considering you started at an A- as part of your penalty, this wasn't so bad. It meant your actual translation was almost mistake-free. It meant you weren't genetically incapable of learning to read, write, and speak this language. And it meant your GPA would stay out of the danger zone for now.

There are no more pranks or acts of sabotage for a while. At least none that you know of. Over the next several days, you get back your first English paper and your Biology quiz, getting a B+ and B respectively. You continue to monitor the gorgeous Connor Blackman online. You find a few more delicious pics of him on the Newland Varsity Soccer team page.

Chloe LaFleur actually smiles at you from her little dorm window, like a beautiful princess in her tower, when you walk by. The weather has grown consistently chilly and the girls who grew up in the northeast say it smells like snow. You can't wait to see the Great Lawn with a fresh blanket of icy powder, drink hot cocoa in front of the fireplace in your dorm commons room, and traipse to class in your brand new blazer and soft, fuzzy mittens.

On Sunday night, Lily Mitchell posts a batch of photos on the Rose House page of The Field. They were taken during the first few days of dorm life. You stare at yourself with your new friends. The pictures make you remember how happy you were just two short weeks ago. Before your stressful class schedule got to you, before missing papers, and missing games. Back when you were filled with that happy sense of anticipation for the future, and your faith that it would all work out.

It's the same mixture of powerful emotions you felt when you tiptoed back up to your room the night you overheard David and Karen talking about sending you back. You knew then, like you do now, that you were going to be okay, somehow. It was that same feeling that drove you to apply to boarding schools and make a new life for yourself. And you did it. You are here.

And it will be that same feeling that makes you decide no one is going to stop you from staying.

Shimmer Journal—

Date/Time: I was getting ready for bed and had to run into my room to write down the shimmer I just had.

Description: I'm standing behind the familiar honey-colored wooden fence that runs the length of Elizabeth's backyard. Even though I'm not physically there, I can feel the force field of energy surrounding her cottage. Suddenly, I hear Elizabeth's distinctive voice. "You're not going to like what I have to say," she announces. "She has the ability — there's no doubt about that. So she's definitely one of us. But I don't think she's...the One."

"How can you be sure?" another woman asks. I don't recognize this second voice. It's high-pitched and strained, like a guitar string pulled taut.

The delicate clinking of tea cups on saucers fills a very long pause. I'm learning to be patient with my visions and let them unfold on their own time. But I'm dying to know who and what they're talking about.

"For one, I asked her several key questions during our first visit, and she scored very low in aptitude. She had several opportunities to use her talents but chose not to. She's either too weak or too scared, and either way, she's not ready. The girl Emma predicted would be so powerful she couldn't hide it or deny it."

"I don't know, Beth, she may just need training," the other voice says skeptically. "Think about it. The environment she grew up in shunned her talents. They were never nurtured. Give her some time to come out of her shell."

"With everything that's happening, we don't have time. You know that," Elizabeth snaps.

I wasn't surprised Elizabeth expects so much so soon from this poor girl, whoever she is. I felt sorry for her. Elizabeth clearly doesn't remember what it's like to be a teenager. The last thing we need at a competitive school is more pressure piled on or another test to fail.

"There's more," she adds. "She's already had an academic misstep. She never turned in her first paper. Winterbourne had a field day. The one we're expecting would never make such a mistake. And she'd know better than to cross Gwendolyn..."

So here's where it gets weird! I suddenly realize Elizabeth is talking about me! She did ask a lot of questions during that first visit. And I'm the only one, as far as I know, who had a late paper. She continued to speak: "Her only responsibility right now is school. Imagine what she'll do once she begins training?" Elizabeth snorts. "Maybe we'll just have to keep looking."

It's so frustrating how vague Elizabeth is. Why can't she just come out and say my name? I have low aptitude for what? And what training? Even as I record this shimmer, there are still so many questions swirling around in my head, it feels like the butterflies found a way in from my stomach.

I wanted to hear more. I wanted to jump over that fence, grab Elizabeth by the shoulders and ask her questions, but the shimmer faded.

Follow Up Comments: I had already brushed my teeth and was just soaping up my face when the shimmer began. The suds were stinging my eyes and the hot water had turned cold by the time it was over. I'm lying in bed now, but I feel wide awake.

You feel restless after writing in your shimmer journal. That strange, long shimmer of Elizabeth's conversation about you gnaws at your brain. You've sent her a written note asking for a face-to-face meeting but she hasn't replied.

You got up several times during the night to look for that damn cricket, the one that moved into Rose House the first day of school. He migrated to the third floor storage closet for a while, then the dorm kitchen, and eventually the bathroom on your floor, where his singing echoed like a soprano in a symphony hall. Gordon Mitchell, George the driver, and even a few of the girls who aren't grossed out by the idea of touching an icky bug tried to catch "Norman" and send him back out into the wild.

About three days ago, Norman decided to take up residence in your bedroom. He chirps mostly at night. His notes bounce into the air thick with brain waves from studying and settle into the billowy folds of your dreams. He occasionally lets out a single, startling chirp during the daylight hours, like a warning shot fired over the bow. Last night he sang from dusk until dawn, and his live concert drove you bananas.

"You look tired," Samantha Carden says as you pass her in the huge, fancy rotunda of the Student Center. She's seated on a plush couch, her legs crossed under her, shoes flipped off onto the floor. A miniature gallery of square slides are scattered on the low table in front of her. Except for not wearing a uniform, she could easily pass for one of the fresh-faced students just hanging out between classes, you think. It's the first time you've seen her since the Winterbourne incident.

You asked around after that and from what you hear, it's hard to say who loves her the most: her Varsity Field Hockey team, the girls who live in her dorm, or the hot-shot finance guy from Boston she's rumored to date. They say he flies up in his helicopter just to take her out to dinner in town. She not a snob like some of the faculty. Other girls say they've seen her out in town having beers with locals. To top it off, every trimester there's a waiting list a mile long for her Art History classes, especially the one she calls Art in the Big Apple. She takes the entire class to New York for a weekend to attend swanky gallery openings and meet the famous painters they're studying.

"I hear you're on the intramural soccer team. How was your game at Archer the other day?" she asks cheerfully. "I saw you jogging across campus in your uniform. Pretty snazzy," she teases.

"You won't believe this..." you say, and then tell her about your latest mishap.

"Wow," she says, letting out a commiserative sigh, her cheeks puffing out like a blowfish. "Pretty nasty prank, I'd say. But I've got a better one," she says. Her even features turn surprisingly fiendish as she talks.

"When I was a Third Former here, we didn't have The Field or IM or any of that. Our mailboxes and that Tyrannosaurus Rex of a Message Board next to the post office was our Internet. I must've checked that thing thirty times a day! Anyway, teachers and coaches left us notes, but so did other girls. One girl even sent a pair of underwear through the mail one time ... "

Your eyes grow big in disbelief.

"Don't ask me why," she chuckles, holding up her hand like a stop sign. "So my field hockey teammates played a prank on me using a fake note in my mailbox too. And to make a long story short, I ended up standing midfield at our first game in a formal gown and heels in front of about three hundred people, including a guy at Newland I had a major crush on! From then on they called me 'Prom Queen.' It was horrific."

"Oh my God!" you laugh, trying to picture Samantha in such a state. She tells you a couple other funny stories about using the mailboxes and Bulletin Board to trick girls into humiliating situations, each one more mortifying than the next. She makes sure to include a note about the rich, famous, fabulous life each victim is now leading. And you get the message. You thank her and head to your next class. You feel lighter, happier, and relieved. It's easy to get caught up in the drama and fear of these weird things that have been happening to you. But she makes it all seem so normal and silly.

But the next time you see Anupa, she has some not-so-normal news.

"Get this," she says, her jewel-toned eyes almost popping out of her head. "Turns out it was easier than I thought to decode the public pathways from here to South Carolina. The invitations the Admin office sent to you for The Field were all intercepted by the same IP address. And I was able to trace it to the town of

Watch Hill, Rhode Island!" She announces this last bit like a reporter with breaking news.

Your mind reels. So there was someone intentionally trying to sabotage you. But who? And why?

"It has to be someone from the school, right?" you say weakly. You wish you had read more Nancy Drew novels when you were little. Your brain is already aching.

"I checked all the student, staff, and faculty files. No one is from that town or even has family there," she says panting. "At least not one that's listed in their files."

"It has to be the same person who hacked in and stole my paper," you say.

"Probably, but I'm still working on that one. The Blackboard stores grades and stuff, so they have it locked down pretty tight."

"Do you think you'll be able to get in?" you say apprehensively, not knowing what you want her answer to be.

Anupa's pensive stare breaks into a cool-headed smirk. "C'mon. It's HTML, not witchcraft," she says shaking her head. "Don't worry, I've got the tools."

Yes she does, you think to yourself. You don't tell Anupa that you know her little secret. That she has her own Internet business selling web design tools to her peers all over the country for their social networking pages and web bio-sites. That she didn't get in on a scholarship like she told you and her parents. That she's made enough ad revenue this month alone to pay for her TW tuition and then some. You know because you shimmered it one day last week after the lunch bell.

At first you were hurt that she wasn't honest with you. Anupa is one of your best friends, and you've shared things with her you've never before said out loud. But then you thought of your own little web of half-truths – about your life, your money, and especially your shimmers. And you realize that you both wanted to escape parents that didn't really get you, a hometown you didn't want to get stuck in, and find a place where you could just be yourself, whatever that means. At this point, you're filled with so many questions and doubts you don't feel like yourself. You've gone from a simple life in a small town to a hotshot boarding school with real enemies. But at least you have Anupa, who you know will work her magic to help you.

That night, you finally sit in the rose and myrrh infused living room at Elizabeth's cottage, after sending another note saying you needed to talk. She got back to you by email with an invitation to dinner. She even got special permission from Gordon and Lily and the Dean to eat dinner at her house. She serves lobster bisque, pot roast, and a salad made entirely from the contents of her garden. This is only your second time to visit her, but every cell in your body rearranges into perfect alignment as soon as you step onto her property. The crazy thoughts and fears ricocheting in your head slow and recede as you sit across from her. Her equanimity is contagious. The two cats recognize you from before and stay by your side throughout dinner.

As you sip your tea and watch Elizabeth perform the most mundane task of stacking logs and kindling to light in her fireplace, you are no less impressed with her. She fascinates you. She's regal. Graceful. Mystical. Strong. But because of her constant line of questioning you don't particularly like her. She reminds you of the doctors and therapists you went to when you were younger, when you were having your "episodes." They, too, were trying to figure something out about you. Scanning your body with their eyes. Reaching inside to peel back the folds of your brain and peer inside. They claimed they just wanted to talk to you. But that was a lie. They were looking for a flaw – a black mark, a malignant stain that would explain why you were you. But they never found what they were looking for in you, and apparently neither did Elizabeth. You desperately want to impress her, and earn her respect, but she always seems slightly disappointed by you.

So when she inquires about your Greek mishap and missing the game, you can't help but blurt out, "Someone is out to get me! I swear!" You clamp your hand over your mouth, but there's no way to stop the tears from forming. One slips halfway down your cheek before you can swipe it away with your free hand.

"Please, dear," she says gently. "Feel free to tell me everything." You have to admit she looks genuinely concerned.

So you tell her the entire story. You find yourself starting all the way back in Hatterly, the night you overheard Karen and David's conversation that sparked your search for a boarding school and take her all the way up to the troubling news you got from Anupa that day. The only thing you can't quite bring yourself to discuss are your shimmers, of course. You use up five Kleenexes and the cats go back into their hiding places, but you don't care. It feels so good to let everything out and to confide in someone. You're not good at lying or even leaving out the truth, so the last few weeks of fudging and fibbing and being only mostly honest with your friends and classmates has been exhausting. Elizabeth asks you several penetrating questions along the way, but she mostly just listens. When you finish, she grows quiet and still. You are sure she is going to send you home – not back to your dorm, back to Hatterly! – for telling her the awful, awkward, troubled truth. But to your surprise, she leans across the table and takes your hand.

"*Sulum Puella Est Donum,*" she says to you solemnly. You remember seeing this Latin phrase for the first time printed on the ornate crest at the top of your acceptance letter, which you keep folded in half in the back of your journal. Since then, you've seen it scrolled across the top of the arching gates as you entered campus, carved into the marble altars and thick stone walls of the chapel, printed across notebooks and folders in the student store, and even stamped faintly on the bottom of your lunch tray when you turn it over to dump your food into the proper composting bin. But when she speaks these words, a shiver runs down your back.

"Every Girl is Gifted," she continues, after catching herself staring pensively into the topaz blue flames burning in her fireplace. "It's the motto of this school. It is the reason it was founded and the principle around which everything was designed. Emma Woodhouse intended this place to be a haven for girls where they can come and not only find that inner light Edith Cadwell was speaking of but discover how to make it brighter. And for many years, everyone who went here, taught here, and worked here was united in this goal."

She looks you directly in the eyes; the power of her gaze paralyzes you. "But, as you know, some girls have talents and abilities that others don't. They are...special. Certain women, myself included, were put in charge of watching for these girls and bringing them to the school. Once here, we give them extra attention to ensure their special gifts are nurtured."

All this talk about abilities and waiting for certain girls they've chosen. Am I one of those "special" girls? Buy how does she know about my shimmering?. And wait, does that mean there are others like me, here at the school? You are dying to ask, the questions burning the tip of your tongue, but you don't dare. You keep your mouth firmly shut just in case she could see the little embers.

She shifts uneasily in her seat, the first time you've seen a crack in her otherwise flawless veneer. "There came a time, as there always does, when the noble fruits of our labor were not sufficient to nourish some of the more acquisitive, power-hungry members of the group. They wanted to pursue a very different agenda. And we divided."

"Is that what the fight at the Headmistress's house was about that day?" you ask.

"Yes," she says, "and Victoria's not even the worst."

There is a crackle by the window and certain parts of the stained glass shift from dark to light. Elizabeth's head whips in that direction, her eyes trained on the same spot as yours. The cats come from their hiding places and pace in front of the window, their tails in the air. It may have been a stray tree branch or bush scraped against the pane by a sudden gust of wind. It may have been the sizzle and popping of the spitting fire. As Elizabeth spoke, its flame burned white hot and cast dancing shadows on the mantel. But you sense Elizabeth is thinking the same thing you are — it looked and sounded as though someone had been standing there. The muscles in Elizabeth's jaw flex and harden, but she maintains her soothing, steady tone.

"My point in telling you all of this is just to say: be careful." She suddenly looks tired, her skin dried out from the fire. Your breath catches in your throat at her ominous warning. "I don't believe you are in any physical danger, but not everyone here can be trusted. You may want to take extra precautions for a little while. Lock your doors, don't leave your things unattended, and for God's sake, don't go into any forbidden areas on campus."

You nod obediently. Then it occurs to you, "But we're not allowed to lock our doors. Third Former rooms don't even have locks," you say, feeling a tremor of panic.

She sighs again. "So they don't. I personally placed you with the Mitchells. They can be trusted. But they cannot be in all places at all times," she says, staring back at the fire. Your curiosity is so strong, it almost gets the better of you, but you stay silent.

Elizabeth walks you home that night. The campus is surprisingly quiet. When you turn out the lights to get in bed, your room looks spooky, like a haunted house. The knobby wood chair legs resemble bones in the pale moonlight. And the darkness forms strange shapes on your wall. A week ago, you suspected someone had been in your room while you weren't there. Your bedspread had an unusual rumple, your alarm clock was turned, and your socks were stuffed under the bed when you came back from dinner. They had been on the floor before you left.

You dismissed it as paranoia. After all, nothing was missing and you don't own anything of value. Your journals lay untouched, wrapped in t-shirts in the back of your drawer. You laptop was closed and it's locked with a password now, thanks to Anupa. But tonight, you think your intuition was right. After Anupa's discoveries and Elizabeth's revelations, you know someone was in your room. Maybe it was the same person who was at Elizabeth's window tonight? You'll have to mention it to Elizabeth the next time you see her.

You pull the covers around you extra tight as Norman begins his moonlight serenade. He's somewhere behind your dresser in between the closets, you can't exactly tell. But tonight you don't mind. You don't stuff your head under your pillow or put your headphones on to muffle the sound. Tonight you lie very still, listening for the hinge of your suite door or footsteps on the path outside your window, and silently start your list of the objects in your room. You're not sure if it's the methodical litany you recite in your head or the comforting companionship of Norman's vibrato, but the next thing you know, you open your eyes and it's morning.

The next day at Friday morning assembly, Dean Acheson announces that another girl is missing a piece of jewelry. This time it's not a gold and diamond daisy necklace, it's a platinum and sapphire bracelet. And this time the rightful owner isn't mousy and pitiful, she's outspoken and pissed!

"Oh my God! That's Anna Seagrave!" Willa gasps, when the fiery brunette with perfectly teased hair swept up in a complicated twist, and a fashionably-wide belt slung loosely over her kilt around her hips, jumps up. "She's the best artist in the school." Willa's eyes are filled with stars and her hands clasped to her chest like a child catching sight of Santa in her living room. You've never seen Willa impressed like this by anyone.

Anna Seagrave is animated with anger. "The last time I had my bracelet was in Art History. I took it off to take my test so it wouldn't knock against the keyboard. So what if I left it in my bag all day? I have a right to do whatever I want with my property without having to worry about some desperate hanger-on pulling a five-finger discount. Anyway, when I got back to my room after all my classes, and dumped out my bag, it was gone!"

"She seems kind of mean," you say as Anna points accusingly at the crowd.

"Oh, she's deplorable," Anupa chimes in. "She is the original mean girl. You should hear her try to order me around, like I'm her personal tech supporter. She thinks the world revolves around her."

"Well it doesn't," Casey hisses. "It revolves around a medium sized, main sequence star that's fading by the minute, so she better wrap it up or I'm gonna be late to Astronomy." She checks her watch impatiently. Casey's got science in the brain. She has a quiz today, which always makes her a little testy, and she likes to follow a very strict schedule she writes out the night before.

Dean Acheson emphasizes that there is no proof that the bracelet was stolen, and until there is, the administration would prefer to assume it is merely lost, or as she calls it "temporarily misplaced." But this is the second piece of expensive jewelry to go missing this year, and as everyone flows out of Assembly, there's a flood of theories about a thief on campus.

It's unsettling, to be sure, but not your biggest concern. Losing precious jewels is luckily one problem you don't have to worry about.

You leave assembly and make a beeline for The Nest to see if your new winter gloves and hat are in.

"Let me check for you, hon. Just a minute," the motherly woman says to you from behind the counter. You turn to peruse the shelves while you wait. Your backpack is bulkier than you realize and it knocks a bin of caterpillar paperweights off the counter. Just before the multi-legged mess hits the floor, a pair of dainty hands appears out of thin air and catches it.

"Whoa. Good catch," you sigh with relief. You didn't think anyone else was in the store. But when you look up, you're less surprised by the feat of superhero speed than you are by the identity of the person who saved the day.

It's Chloe LaFleur.

Your guard flies back up and you look away.

"De rien," she sings.

You give a quick smile and nod as you slip into the aisle of books and journals, grateful to escape having to stand awkwardly beside the ice queen. She's even more perfect up close than from a distance, and it's intimidating. But to your surprise, Chloe follows you!

"You're Elizabeth Wilmington's friend, right?" she asks. Her accent is so thick it sounds like she's invented her own language.

"She's my advisor, yeah," you reply. Curiosity ripples over you as you recall Elizabeth asking you about Chloe as well.

"Isn't she a fantastic woman?" she asks moving so close, you can smell the pineapple milkshake in her hand. She has picked up a package of bear-shaped wafers and nibbles on one as she talks. It's the first time you've seen her eat anything besides her signature candies, but it's still pure sugar.

"Yeah. How do you know her?" you ask, starting down the book aisle.

"She went to school here with my American Grandmere," Chloe answers.

"Have you read Griffin and Sabine?" Chloe takes a book from the shelf and opens it.

"No, I've never heard of it."

"It is the most wonderful story about two artists who find one another and share a metaphysical connection, even though they are half a world apart." Chloe flips open the beautifully illustrated book and pulls a folded piece of paper from a hand-decorated envelope on the inside. Her red nails blaze against the brown pages. "See? The story unfolds through the letters, postcards, and notes they exchange, and you get to read each one. It's like going through someone else's mail," she adds with a wink.

Where did this girl come from? You wonder. She's so cool.

"Sounds voyeuristic," you mumble, pulling the book towards you for a better look.

Chloe's lips curve into a bewitching smile.

"Yes, but it's also about taking a chance, a challenge to reach out across space and over time to make a friend. Griffin and Sabine are soul mates, and these are the keepsakes of their friendship," she explains, her inflection rising and falling like a ballerina on the clouds. Her gaze is steady and the spirit in her eyes makes you feel like you are old friends. As she goes on to tell you about her dog Piccolo and her childhood friend from home, you realize she's not the cold-hearted recluse that everyone, including you, thinks she is. She's just a girl.

She notices the time and has to dart away. She gives you a quick peck on each cheek, French-style, and is gone as quickly as she came. Little clumps of crumbs on the floor are the only evidence of your strange encounter with the Chloe kind.

You drift back up to the counter where your new cashmere mittens and matching hat are waiting. You charge them and the first book of the trilogy of Griffin and Sabine to your account and begin reading as you walk home.

The next day, Saturday, is the first day Third Formers are allowed off campus and the entire class is going on its first trip of the year to Boston.

Boston!

Home of the flagship Urban Outfitters, Newbury Comics, and the Boston Art Museum, which is temporarily housing an exhibit from one of the few artists Willa doesn't have to explain to you: Claude Monet. You're obsessed with his "Water Lilies." Everyone's going — all of your friends. And word has it from the highest sources (Willa) that Newland is sending two busloads too.

Everyone will be there, that is, except you.

Instead, thanks to the soccer "prank" and your whopping 55 demerits, you will be sitting in the stuffy old Counting House stuffing envelopes while your friends are in Beantown. Just your luck. What if Connor is there? Even if you didn't catch sight of his glorious face, you'd love to see the city and run around with your friends.

"It's going to be so much fun," Casey moans. "I wish you were coming!"

"I know," you grumble as you watch her and Willa pack their backpacks.

"It's a good thing you're going as a gypsy for Halloween. That makes it easy to pick stuff out for you. Don't worry, we'll bring you good pieces," Willa offers sincerely. They were all going to hunt for Halloween costumes for the upcoming parties and the dance the school hosts with Newland on the last day of the month.

"Thanks," you say, feeling sorry for yourself. You were planning on looking for some souvenirs to decorate your room as well as your uniform. For the first time, you actually have money to spend, but you can't even enjoy it. And more than the actual objects, you want the experience and memories of going to the city, being with your friends, flirting with boys, and shopping for yourself. As they drive off in boisterous buses, you trudge to the Counting House where Mrs. Dunahoo, the Alumni Director, is waiting for you and two other girls who also have sentences to serve.

"Here are your materials. Please remember why you are here. This is not social hour. You are here to do a job and the job better be well done. These envelopes are going out to distinguished alumni all over the world. So no funny business," she warns with a wag of her finger. She sets you up at a long wooden table with bins and buckets overflowing with papers. The school spared no expense to design and create special pamphlets adorned with ritzy pictures of the school, the students, and past events. They are printed on special thick paper as soft as satin. There are 2400 in all. And it takes you all day to count, collate, fold, stuff, and lick each little package and place them in their proper bins.

At five o'clock, just as you are placing the stamp on your last envelope, Regan Jenner comes rolling into the back office of the Counting House where you and your cellmates are sitting. You haven't seen her in almost three weeks, since that first day.

"Hey there, you!" she says. She has a steaming cup of hot chocolate in each hand. Her cashmere camel scarf is coiled around her neck like a stack of doughnuts. The two other girls glance at her disinterestedly and begin to clean up their workspaces. "I stayed back to break in my new roller blades. Samantha told me you were stuck here today. So she asked me to drop in and see how it's going."

Even Samantha Carden went to Boston, you think grimly. She invited you to join her group for lunch at the Institute of Contemporary Art in the seaport district. It was nice of her to send Regan to check on you. But right now, you nervously eye the melted cocoa and milk sloshing around the edge of the cup she carries.

"Thanks, Regan. But we're just finishing up," you say amiably. You lurch forward reflexively when Regan wavers a little on her skates. But she rights herself and never misses a beat.

"Okay then! I'm off! Gotta run this hot chocolate over to Monica Brewster. She's got the flu and I..whooo...Whoa...Whoa!" GOOSH! Regan loses her balance, upending both cups. You watch as two large chocolate streams sail through the air and land all over the freshly stuffed envelopes neatly lined up in little rows across the table. "Oh my goodness! I'm so sorry! I'm such a goof!" Regan wails. You and the two other girls leap up and try to salvage some of the envelopes just as Mrs. Dunahoo comes down the hall.

"What is this? Some kind of party?" she squawks as she enters the room. But when she looks down and sees the soggy rows of envelopes splashed with dark brown spots, she grows incensed. She stalks around the room surveying the damage. Regan ruined over half of the envelopes. And you can't tell if the steam filling up the room is from the puddles of hot chocolate or Mrs. Dunahoo's ears.

"Regan, you should know better," she scolds. "Please leave at once." Regan rolls out of the room looking guilty. "As for the three of you, you will have to come back tomorrow to re-do all of these packets."

"But what about Regan? She's the one who spilled," Robin Swanson has the guts to say as Mrs. Dunahoo is leaving the room. But Robin moves behind her chair when she turns on her heels to address her.

"This was your responsibility. The three of you. Not Regan's. You shouldn't have invited her. I told you no funny business," she chides and flies out of the room before anyone else can object, not that anyone would.

As you emerge from the Counting House, the campus is like a ghost town. The shuttles are not back from Boston. And the only people in sight are a couple of groundskeepers in the distance raking the fall foliage into little orange, red, and yellow mounds. A wintry wind whips through trees and undoes their afternoon of work. I know exactly how that feels, you think to yourself. Two black crows land on one of the picnic tables on the Great Lawn and pick at a piece of pale green, dried gum. You've always liked crows, ever since you were researching a Halloween report on Pagan rituals for your seventh grade history class and you read they are supposed to be highly psychic. But you also read crows are omens of doom and death. So you shoo them away as you pass by.

You check your watch. 5:45. The shuttles aren't due back for another hour. The only thing left to do is check your mail. Even the post office seems strangely desolate. You expect to see a tumbleweed blow through the halls like in those old Westerns you used to watch on Saturday mornings at the girls' home. There is the upcoming week's menu. To your delight, there is also a violet envelope with vaguely familiar handwriting. You rip it open. It's invitation from Samantha Carden! Even her handwriting is cool. In funky purple ink, she wrote: "Hey Girl! Thought you could use some R&R after all that demerit work today. Come to my house tomorrow evening for a little M&M – movie and a makeover! See ya then! P.S. Dinner included. I've already cleared it with the Mitchells."

You can't wait for this wretched day to be over. At least now you have something to look forward to.

Your stomach is growling as you enter your bedroom and toss your backpack on your bed. But you don't want to eat alone in an empty dining hall with nothing but the sound of your own chewing to keep you company. So you decide to wait for your roommates to return. You make sure to tack Samantha's invite onto your bulletin board with one of the 3-D ladybug pins you bought at the Nest. They make you smile every time you look at their buggy little eyes and daintily dotted shells.

After rummaging through the pile of books and papers that accumulates on your desk like a lint trap in a dryer that must be cleaned out each week, you locate your list of homework. If you're going to be spending Sunday evening at Samantha's, you can't afford to leave all of your assignments until tomorrow. But nothing from this menu looks appetizing – one hundred and ten pages for your Sacred Texts class, forty equations to proof in Pre-Calculus, a set of follow-up questions from Friday's lab in

Biology, another brain boggling Greek translation, shorter than the first.

It's like staring at a plate of cauliflower when all your want is a cheeseburger. You pull your laptop in front of you and take a moment to run your hand over its smooth silver cover.

You get online and go straight to Chloe's LaFleur's page. Reading Chloe's poems and staring at her fantastical photos has been a hobby of yours since you saw her bodyguards on the Great Lawn that first day. If you click through the pictures fast enough, you feel like you're skipping through her glamrock life with her, wind in your face, head thrown back in delirious laughter, like the image of her with some friends at Mardi Gras.

The first time you saw her page, you were sitting with Anupa in the computer lab. She was giving you a private tutorial of The Field so you could trick out your own page a little more.

"If you pay attention and don't interrupt, I'll show you some insider info on the system," she teased, flicking your hand lightly with a ruler. "But remember, with great information comes great responsibility..." she warbled, doing her best school marm impression. As she clicked over the profiles to get to your page, she happened to stop on Chloe's.

"Whoa," was all Anupa could say. It was rare she was at a loss for words, but that's what Chloe does to people. In addition to her eye-catching background, Chloe was staring back at you from all over the page, her signature, fire engine red lipstick and nails lighting up every frame. Her starlet hair was perfectly coiffed even when she's stretched out on the beach or laying in bed. Anupa used Chloe's page as an example to show you various features of The Field and ways you can enhance your site because Chloe had done them all.

"What are those little emoticons in the Posting Column?" you asked.

"That's weird. I've never seen anonymous messages on The Field before. You have to enter a screen name and school just to get in," Anupa explained. She was clearly intrigued. She read a few of the mystery postings out loud:

"I know how your mother died, and who did it. Watch out, or you'll follow in her footsteps."

"If you're having trouble sleeping it's because my spell is working."

"Nice pictures, babe, but you'd look a lot better locked up in my attic."

"Ew. Those postings are creepy!" you shriek.

"Yup. And mean. Freaks and Geeks. They're on every block in every city. Just be glad you can't see them. They're probably sitting in their tighty whities playing Worlds of Wisards," Anupa said causally clicking off Chloe's page and bringing up your own.

"It's the dark side of the otherwise enlightening internet," she announces with authority.

Tonight you don't bother with sinister messages from other readers, you simply stare at the life Chloe has captured on screen and the one you've been creating in your mind. In one picture, the caption "Points de Polka et Rayons de Lune," Chloe looks like a cotton candy machine has swallowed her whole. "Polka Dots and Moonbeams Party," you translate out loud with only minor difficulty. Your French Professor Madame Baldur would be pleased with your progress. Chloe swims in bustled tiers of fluffy satin, poofy netting, and lace. She's clutching a champagne flute in one hand and a red rose in the other as a handsome boy in a tuxedo kisses her rouged cheek. Her eyes are squinting with delight.

But the carefree spirit captured in the thumbnail photos from fancy parties, beach bonfires, and blurred out acts of impropriety with celebrities stand in stark contrast to her evocative poetry. And now that you've talked to the girl behind the images, the words take on a whole new meaning.

With titles like "A Heart Too Heavy To Lift," "Some Karma Love," and "Men and Mayonnaise," Chloe gets down and dirty with love, heartache, sex, drugs, partying, death, parents, fame, and, yes, spirituality. You read through one called 'No Mother, No Problem," and learn her mom died when she was six. And by the sounds of "The Not So Merry Go Round," her dad would rather date teenage girls than spend time with his own.

Anupa refers to Chloe as the Parisian Princess with a Heart. You can't tell if it's a cut down or compliment coming from her but you know you feel more empathy for Chloe than Anupa ever could. You know what it's like to feel lonely, unwanted and unsure. But more than that, you sense a special bond with Chloe that defies logic. It was there in your shimmers, in your dreams, and at the Nest.

Chloe hasn't posted many pictures since she came to TW – only one or two close-ups that she took of herself. But her oeuvre of expression has grown by leaps and bounds. Your favorite things are her poems. And her latest one almost makes you fall out of your chair.

Send a message; take a chance.
A true friend is waiting to connect.
We come from different worlds to this magical place
But we have more in common than you suspect.

I know about dreamlike visions festooned with doubt
A past you'd rather not say
Gifts you wish you could give back
But they make you who you are today

Hold the phone! Your mind may be numb from counting envelopes all day, but it sounds like she's talking about you. Even *to* you. But how could that be? You did share that weird moment in your shimmer when it seemed like she could sense you were with her, watching her. But that would mean she had some kind of ability too. Maybe that's what she means by knowing dream-like visions? But how does she know about your past?

Maybe you should email her, you think to yourself.

"Send a message. Take a chance," you say out loud, your voice breaking the silence of your room. It's something you've wanted to do ever since you first visited her virtual world and especially after yesterday's encounter. Chloe followed you, and she was genuinely friendly. Now this poem – she's practically calling out to you.

You sit down to type, but two seconds later, you hear a rumble below. They're back from Boston. Moments later, Willa and Casey come crashing into the suite and barging into your room. Chloe will have to wait.

They are alive with stories from their day in the city, and they have costumes, and presents, and trinkets to show you.

"Are you ready to see what you'll be donning on All Hallow's Eve?" Willa asks digging in her bag. "For just one night, you will be instantly transformed into Esmerelda, the temptress of Trumbull Woodhouse!" She purs with a sultry Romanian accent. She unfurls a billowy-sleeved white peasant blouse and a striking crimson shawl. Next to it she lays the most gorgeous cobalt blue skirt exploding with little gold lame flowers.

"Ooooh," "oh," "ahhhh," and "wow" are suddenly the only words in your vocabulary. Casey stands nearby, fanning her hands over the pieces, drawing your attention to details, like a young Vanna White.

"And this is for your head." she adds pulling out an asparagus green head scarf with octagonal little mirrors dangling from the fabric. She even managed to find a Roman Coin belt to drape across your waist and little gold slippers that totally complete the look. She had thought of everything. "Doesn't it just scream 'gypsy'?" Willa insisted, her eyes lighting up with excitement.

"Willa, it's perfect! You have really outdone yourself!" you exclaim and give her a big hug.

"Oh! And look what I got off an artist in Harvard Square for four bucks! I thought of you when I saw it cause I know you have a thing for stars," she adds with a gentle elbow to the ribs as though you two have your own little secret.

"It's beautiful! I love it!" you sigh. And it was. Leave it to Willa to pick out the perfect little painting of a misty, magical meadow at night with a full moon and canopy of twinkling stars in a blue black sky. You know just the spot for it on your wall, next to your bed.

Casey and Willa brought back a pizza to share, and the three of you can't wait to chow down. But first, you IM Anupa to invite her over for a carpet picnic, ignoring Casey's eye rolls that are so dramatic her eyeballs practically pop out of their sockets. By the time Anupa flops on the floor next to you, you've heard a minute by minute account of their day.

"We had lunch with a bunch of boys from Newland, friends of Everett's," Casey chuckles.

This reminds you of someone you do want to ask about. "Was

hottie-von-hotterson there?" you ask, referring to Connor Blackman of course. They all know who you mean, but no one says a word. The room suddenly goes quiet. Like synchronized eaters, they all shove a bit of pizza into their mouths at once, their eyes darting from face to face as they chew slowly.

"Well, Connor was there..." Willa says cautiously around a giant bite. You can tell there's a 'but.' There's always a but. "But you're not gonna like who was flirting with him," she says, her face scrunching up at the thought.

"Who?" you say weakly, afraid for her to continue. Your stomach and the two ooey-gooey slices of three cheese pizza you've eaten, do a back flip at the thought of anyone flirting with him at all. But the "who" makes it worse.

"You tell her. I can't," Willa says, covering her eyes and rolling up into a little ball on the floor waiting for the fallout. Casey looks at Anupa.

"It was the Little Miss Manners in there," Anupa says dryly. That's her nickname for Hayden ever since she ran into her coming out of the computer lab. Hayden was staring at a picture of herself and her friends from New York, and she ran right into Anupa who was carrying a stack of papers she'd just organized. The papers went flying and so did Anupa right on her tailbone.

"Are all computer freaks as clutzy as you?" Hayden said haughtily as she straightened her skirt. As she sauntered off, she made sure to step on the scattered papers and gave an extra twist of her heel to shred them in half.

Your heart sinks. "Was he flirting back?" you ask and they nod yes. "Whatever," you say trying to sound strong, but your voice sounds thin like tinfoil and you fee like crying. "He's rich and handsome and dates supermodels. And Hayden is the next best thing, I guess." But the part you're not saying, that you don't have to guess, is that you could never live up to that.

"Supermodel Schmupermodel," Casey says. "The girl is overrated."

"Yeah, more like beauty school drop out," Anupa quips crossing her arms and smirking at Hayden's closed bedroom door.

"Yeah, and there were like nine other girls vying for his attention," Willa declares. "He was paying attention to everyone and no one, if you know what I mean."

And you did, but it doesn't make the bitter taste of envy that's pooled in your mouth go away. Not even the pizza can mask it. You take a swig of soda to try and clear it out, but it takes all night to fade.

When you wake up the next morning, the first thing you see is your little painting of the moon, and you smile. It was the last thing you looked at before falling asleep. And you slept deeply, despite Norman's constant chirping. You feel rested even though you stayed up past 2 AM to finish most of your homework. It's funny how a good night's sleep, and the anticipation of a night with two of your favorite people can make everything seem okay. You found out last night that Willa was invited to Samantha's too. She is Samantha's pet art history student, so it didn't surprise you, and you can't think of a better person to share the evening with.

You sit up and pull your laptop in bed with you. The cold October air whistling through the casement windows makes it hard to justify sitting at your desk when you can stay snuggled under your covers. The suite is quiet. You must be the first to start your Sunday morning. You check your email while you wait for the others to rise. The first message is from Mrs. Dunahoo – there goes your glorious morning. You read her message out loud to wake up your voice.

"Attention girls: The Alumnae Office has to print up more fundraiser materials, which won't arrive for at least a week. Your disciplinary obligation will be delayed until then. Regards, Mrs. Dunahoo."

Hooray! Yahoo! Yiiipppeee! Dungeon duty has been delayed! You spring out of bed with a sudden burst of energy. You stretch to get the kinks out, but you already feel light and nimble without the weight of 2400 envelopes and Mrs. Dunahoo's beady eyes boring down on you.

After you finish your conjugations for French and check over your Greek, you and Willa decide to explore the campus and go for a long walk before heading over to Samantha's. You invited Casey, but she has to chair her environmental club meeting, and you haven't seen Anupa today. She usually holds an open tutoring session in the computer lab on Sundays. So the two of you bundle up and walk past the Rose Garden, through the Upper Field, and into the forest at the base of Trumbull Hill.

"Did you hear Carden has a love nest tucked away in town?" Willa asks you as you hike through the trees. The fallen leaves are damp underfoot. The air is thick with frost and you can see Willa's breath escape from her mouth in little white puffs.

"No!," you gasp. "How do you know?"

"Alexis Pratt told me on the shuttle yesterday." Willa says, running her tongue over her teeth at the juicy news.

You point at Willa and snicker. "So you were Hayden's stand-in for the day?" you tease.

Willa rolls her eyes at the ongoing Alexis saga. Last month Alexis was a loyal member of team Murdoch. And she worked hard to keep up with Hayden's rules – like not wearing yellow on Thursdays or orange ever, leaving your hair down on Fridays, and waiting for the weekend she assigned to you to wear jeans. But in spite of a perfect performance, Hayden turned on her for no reason and iced her out. And she's ordered her henchmen to keep Alexis in her place with deafening silence and death glares that shoot daggers right through her.

At first Alexis was crushed. She wrote Danielle a note begging her to explain what she'd done, but Danielle posted it on the bulletin board in the mailroom for everyone to see. That night, Alexis had an anxiety attack and spent the next two days in the Infirmary. But once she realized the mean girl monster has many heads, she had a newfound hope. (Her new Prozac prescription probably helped too.)

"She claims she's 'bonding, big-time' with Rachel Strauss and her followers, so she should have a new home soon. But can we get back to the good stuff?" Willa begs. "Supposedly Samantha shacks up there with her big city boyfriend when he comes to town."

"She is such a rock star!" you reply. This news only makes Samantha seem even more exotic and daring in your eyes.

"I know," Willa agrees with a little chuckle. The two of you hike on through the damp, chilly woods. The cold air is invigorating and before you know it, you've hiked all the way to the base of Arcadia Mountain. It looms ominously against the pale blue sky. Slate grey storm clouds sit heavily over its peak.

"I've never been all the way over here before," Willa says, a little out of breath. "It's pretty," she says glancing around. The woods have grown quiet, just the occasional pop or crackle as the trees wake up and stretch their limbs. But for some reason, the birds have stopped talking to each other. An old stone wall rises from the uneven terrain and meanders along the edge of the forest as far as you can see. It is so quiet and isolated, it's possible to imagine you are in a different time. And for just a moment, you close you eyes and let your imagination run wild. But Willa's grip on your arm startles you.

"What is that?" she asks, pointing to a two story stone building in the distance.

"I don't know," you reply pulling out your map of campus. But it's not on your map. And it's not on Willa's either.

"That's weird," she says, her mouth shifting to the side in a mischievous grin. "Let's go check it out," she whispers as she pulls you with her towards the ominous building.

You let her take you, but Elizabeth's warnings echo in your brain. And suddenly, another pair of crows squawk loudly from a branch overhead. You look around for a minute, your feet still moving under you, and you realize those are the only birds around, the first ones you've seen in awhile. You think you see the silhouette of a person behind one of the trees. But no, maybe it's just a shadow? A chill runs through your bones making you shudder, and it's not from the snow that's in the forecast. Your hands reflexively reach up and pull your fleece jacket around you tighter, your pace slowing to a stop.

"What's wrong?" Willa asks, oblivious to the menacing thoughts filling your head.

"Oh, nothing, I just think we should head back. We don't want to be late to Samantha's," you say nonchalantly.

"Oh!" she says disappointedly. But then, to your relief, she changes her mind. "You're right," she says. "I want to grab a few brushes to bring to Samantha's. But we're definitely coming back to check this place out."

Over my dead body, you think. You wish you could have the

carefree curiosity that Willa has, but all you can think is that somebody is out to get you. He or she could be lurking in the shadows or around any corner.

Forty minutes later, you knock on Samantha Carden's door. Six o'clock on the dot. She lives on the top floor of Moser Hall. The school converted an entire suite into one giant apartment for her when she arrived. She answers the door in flowing ivory-colored pants and a lavender camisole with a cashmere sweater thrown over it. Her sophisticated outfit carries over into her décor. You step into her incredibly chic menagerie; it's better than you ever imagined. You knew her invite was a coveted golden ticket. But you never thought you'd want to run through her house touching, tasting, and smelling everything in sight like the children in the chocolate factory.

Just standing in the entryway, you can see that the suite is a trove of color-drenched rooms, filigree shelves, and elegant antiques. A wonderful mixture of smells wafts in from the kitchen – tomato, oregano, and cooking cheese.

"I'm making lasagna. I heard it was your favorite," she says with a huge grin. Mary Kate was right that first day on the way to school – everyone knows everything about everyone at this place. But you're so enamored by her apartment and enchanted by the whole experience, you don't care.

As the dutiful host, she gives you a quick tour – living room, office, bedroom, "powder room," and a small dining nook. All of the rooms have a French deco vibe, right down to the retro silver vanity next to her bed. Each room has different textiles, but they all share the same fresh palette of powder blues, bone and khaki, and rich chocolate browns. Bold lamps stationed on every table give off a soft glow as the three of you plop down on her rich wool rug.

"I've had these since college," she says pointing to the blue goblets you're sipping seltzer from. "I was visiting my brother who lives in Paris with his second wife, but I got locked out of their apartment. I was furious with myself, but it turned out to be the best day ever. I had no choice but to stroll around the city until they came home. I found these in an outdoor antique market I stumbled upon towards the end of the day."

It sounds like something you'd read in a travel magazine, but no, it was her life.

"Do you have any other siblings?" Willa asks wistfully seeming just as impressed by the story as you are.

"Nope, just a brother. But we're very close. I wish he didn't live so far away."

"And what about your parents?" you ask wanting to know every detail of her history, and take notes on every minute since she was born.

"My mother lives in San Francisco, and we are best friends. My father lives closer, but I try to avoid him." She takes a big gulp from her goblet filled with Chardonnay. "They divorced when I was eight, and my mother became very depressed. She didn't get out of bed for six months straight. She lost her job, and couldn't afford to keep our home or take care of my brother and me. We were living in Massachusetts at the time and the state came and took us away. My brother and I were placed in different foster homes. It was horrible and very traumatic. It took my mom two years to get back on her feet, but as soon as she was, we were all reunited."

She tells the story as though the ordeal she went through was as common as earaches and chicken pox.

You stare at her in awe. Shock and awe. The ticker tape of thought running through your head says one thing: Samantha

Carden was a foster kid, just like you! Sure, she has a mom and dad, and even a real brother, but she was there – those smelly rooms, that little bed, those lonely nights. She knows. This is the closest you've come to knowing someone like you who you like. And you really, really like her. You don't want to just know her, you want to be her. She went to Princeton and traveled all around the world. She's lived in foreign cities, and attended posh parties. She has friends, and family. She has her own beautiful boyfriend and impeccable knowledge of art, architecture, literature, music, fashion, and design that tumbles from her mouth, hangs from her walls, sits on her shelves, wafts through the air, threads through her clothes, and shines in her eyes.

It is an empowering realization that bonds you to Samantha like glue. She will forever be the first person who made you feel you could have a life like this. Even if you were an orphan, you could belong. And for the rest of the night you are sitting on top of a cloud, watching from above as you, Willa, and Samantha eat delicious lasagna, make a lighter than air meringue pie, paint each other's nails, try on Samantha's clothes, and dye Willa's hair. It takes so long, you don't even get to the movie part of the evening, but you don't even notice.

It is a make-over that would go down in the history books, or at least your journal entry that night. Willa is going as Andy Warhol for Halloween, a costume that requires her to go a few shades lighter to platinum blonde. Most people would have just settled for a wig, too afraid to commit to a decision so permanent or a color so bold. But not Willa.

"Blondes have more fun, right?" she says puckering her lips and shrugging her shoulders as Samantha applies the pungent peroxide. "The brighter the blonde, the more the fun," she announces happily.

All eyes were on Willa and her new hair at Monday morning assembly. Overnight her hair had taken on a glowing sheen, as though she dipped her head in moon dust. You knew in a matter of days there would be several more dye jobs popping up around campus as girls tried to replicate her punk couture aesthetic. Dean Acheson normally runs things at the Assembly but, to everyone's surprise, Madame Cadwell steps up to the lectern. Her lips purse in a thin line as the Headmistress gazes out at her girls. Dean Acheson and the three other deans, whom you haven't seen since Convocation, are standing behind her. They have equally sour expressions.

"Whoa. This must be serious," Casey whispers.

"This is gonna be good," you hear Alexis Pratt hiss four bodies away.

The room goes quiet when Madame Cadwell clears her throat. "A pair of diamond earrings have disappeared from Moser

Hall," she begins solemnly. "They were in Claudia Everheart's jewelry box inside her dresser when she went to dinner last night, but they were gone when she went to put them on this morning." She pauses and takes a deep breath before continuing.

She's the only one in the room who is breathing at the moment. No one else would dare to miss a single word of what she will say next. "We now have reason to believe there is a pattern of missing items sufficient to suspect a thief on campus."

A clatter reverberates off the walls and around the room as hundreds of girls' jaws drop to the hardwood floor. Their eyes are fixated on Madame Cadwell, like a bunch of ventriloquist dummies waiting for someone to animate them. "If you have any information or saw anything suspicious in Moser Hall or any of the residential units, please report it to me or one of the Deans at once."

You and Willa were in Moser Hall last night for your M&M with Samantha, but you don't recall seeing anyone in the dorm. Everyone was at dinner and then in study hall. Willa must've been thinking the same thing as she leans forward and mouths to you "Did you see anything?" You shake your head no and try to shrug it off. But you wish your heart would stop beating so fast, as if it knows something you don't. Something it has obviously told your stomach, which is churning at this very moment.

"Lack of trust is one the most insidious and degrading forces to the fabric of a small community like Trumbull Woodhouse. And anyone who possesses and acts on the compulsion to steal, especially from their sisters here at school, needs help. And we would like to get them the appropriate treatment," the Headmistress continues.

She went on to instruct everyone to store their valuables in the dorm safes or with their dorm parents, and assured everyone this would be cleared up soon "one way or another." She gives a curt smile and nods before ending her speech, but nothing about her tone or demeanor is reassuring.

Your hands and feet feel hot and your face is flushed in spite of the chilly mid-morning air as you walk to class. You know you didn't do anything wrong, but there's something that bothers you about the whole thing. Your brain itches. It wants you to scratch it but you are afraid of what you may find underneath. Your intuition is telling you something, but you can't or don't want to hear it. Instead, you focus on the snippets of accusations and speculation from the girls in your history class as you settle into your desk.

"Maybe she's been a closet kleptomaniac her whole life," Marion Fisher posits about the thief, her bundle of straw colored hair bushy around her face.

"But what is she gonna do with the jewelry? It's not like she can wear it around campus," Julianna Theophilus points out to her group of friends.

"Maybe she'll hock 'em on e-Bay," Amber Gifford replies.

"Oooh, good one," a voice says from a girl who is sitting behind you.

You have a rancid taste in your mouth and your stomach is officially sour, as if the bands of nervous energy buzzing through campus since Madame Cadwell's announcement caused the glass of milk you had this morning to curdle. You sit at your desk and try to focus on the murmur of gossip whirring around the room instead of the white frothy foam rising in your throat. And then comes the ultimate distraction – a shimmer.

You suddenly find yourself in someone's living room. The massive fireplace is casting a warm, orange glow on the rose colored walls. You are not anywhere on TW's campus, that's for sure. A woman is talking on the phone. And although you can't see her face, you are almost certain it's Samantha. Her voice sounds strained and craggy, like she swallowed a bag of broken glass. But it's still her. But these low beamed ceilings and that winding narrow staircase in the corner – where is she? You wonder.

"Listen, I'm tired of playing it safe," she barks. "We've thrown up roadblock after roadblock, and she's stumbled, but it's time to take her down once and for all. She already has her little friend snooping around for her. And I don't think we can afford to wait any longer. With your permission, I'll see to it this little game ends in our favor."

At first you thought she was talking about field hockey. But that doesn't sound like the game she's discussing. You confided in her last night about your suspicion that someone had been in your room. And you mentioned Anupa was following up on the electronic snafus. Thank God you didn't go into any detail. Samantha seemed genuinely concerned and promised to watch your back, which made you feel safe. But now you are confused. You may not have these shimmers figured out but you know your brain is showing you this for a reason. You feel a piercing pain in your heart, but it's not indigestion. Samantha peels a throaty cackle into the phone. It bellows in your ears and echoes in your skull. A sick feeling of betrayal and regret rises from the pit of your stomach and into your mouth.

Your shimmer fades and class is already in session. You try to concentrate on the lecture, but the shimmer leaves a black residue on your tongue and your lips. You run to the bathroom to rinse it away.

You stumble through the rest of your day in a daze, dropping your tray on the floor in the dining hall when you completely miss your chair going to sit. You end up splayed out on the floor next to a leaf of lettuce and an overturned bun from the hamburger that was supposed to be your lunch. Alexis Pratt looks over and mistakes the ketchup on your palms and shirt as something more threatening and screams out "Ohmygosh! She's bleeding!" Everyone turns to stare and the staff rushes over, causing a scene.

You trip as you walk into Professor Peirce's class, stubbing your toe on his obnoxiously large oak desk. "Ow, ow, ow, ow, ow!" you repeat clutching your foot.

"Can you try not to be such a spaz?" Tina Spurlock, a mini Halle Berry from New York crows from the front row.

"Gotcha!" Maggie Hornbach whoops as she strips the ball right out from under you at soccer practice that afternoon.

Maggie is the worst defender on the intramural team, which means she must be bad – the worst of the worst. And even she is surprised how easy it was to steal the ball away. She stops a few steps downfield, blinking rapidly, waiting to see if it's some kind of trick.

When you get back to your room, Casey is waiting for you in the doorway. "Hey! You gotta see this! I was looking at the – whoa." She stops and stares at you with concern. "You look…weird. Are you feeling ok?"

You walk right past her and crawl into bed, not bothering to smile or talk. "I just have a really bad headache – maybe getting the flu," you say absentmindedly and roll over. You turn your back on her, and the room, and this awful day. "What did you want to show me?"

She hesitates for a moment but decides to back off. "Never mind. It's probably nothing. It can wait until you feel better. I have some Advil if you need it," she says and turns off your light to let you rest.

You wish it was that simple. You'd give anything to merely be suffering from cramps or a fever. You're thinking about that knob that was turned up on the volume of the world – on your ability to hear the essence of people and things – like a drop of water evaporating in a coffee pot or a mosquito landing on the sill. After Madame Cadwell's morning announcement and the Samantha shimmer, that knob is cranked up so high it's impossible for you to think about or focus on anything else. If you close your eyes and just let go, there's an underlying rhythm, an undeniable message from the universe beat out in Morse code.

Once you are under the covers, under the pillows, under the white orb of the moon and the confetti stars, you try to go to the one reliable place that is quiet – sleep. But there isn't much comfort there either. You toss and turn, The only two visions you have are more like shimmers than dreams because you never really fall asleep. And both are disturbing.

The first one is the old familiar – an unknown hand writing your name in the unknown book. But in tonight's version, when your name is complete, she crosses it off. The ink turns blood red and fiery, a venomous snake unleashed from the pen. And the corners of the page glow and smolder, curling and peeling until the paper is consumed by an invisible flame. The sounds of gushing, rushing, crackling, howling, and clamoring fills the room. The next thing you know you are tumbling, head over feet, in a spin cycle of darkness. You can't see anything but you can feel a presence in the space. Someone is standing over you, watching you. Is this just part of your shimmer or is this really happening?

Your eyes pop open, your hand reaches for the light. It's 5 AM. The noise in your head recedes to a low din and your brain itches again with a message you cannot decipher. You are alone in your room in the gray-brown light just before dawn. It's still and quiet.

Too quiet, in fact. Where's Norman? He isn't singing like he always is by now, not even a warning bell or chirp from his corner of the room. You slip out of bed onto your hands and knees, not sure why you're so desperate to find this little creature. And then you see him.

Someone was in your room, all right. Norman's skeleton has been crushed by a shoe that left a print on your floor. There's only half a print in the dust, so you can't tell what kind, but it really doesn't matter. It tells you everything you need to know just by being there. There are several more prints in the common room too. Someone could argue they are from any of your roommates' shoes or even yours, but you know better. Nothing is just a coincidence anymore, not for you and not at this school. And nothing surprises you these days.

Including the timing of the transformation that is taking place within you. You should be terrified at the thought of someone sneaking into your room. Or paralyzed with fear that you are in someone's crosshairs. But you feel surprisingly calm. All of those jangly nerves and dizzying doubts since these mysterious mishaps began are beginning to organize. They are hardening into a little army of pluck and indignation and lining up along your backbone making you strong.

Willa is waiting for you after Greek; her face is ashen. "Have you checked your email or your mailbox today?" Her voice is high pitched and wobbly.

"No why?" you ask coolly.

"Dean Acheson wants to see us."

"Right now?"

"Yeah. They've been interviewing girls all morning," she explains, wringing her hands. "I know we didn't do anything wrong, but I have a bad feeling," she says, gulping hard. Something inside you knew this was coming.

When you arrive at Dean Acheson's office, Hayden is just leaving. She bumps you hard as she passes you in the doorway.

"Looks like I'll be getting that corner room after all," she breathes into your ear. "I knew you didn't belong here." She blows you a kiss and blazes out. You stop and stare back at her, indignation coursing through your veins. You knew she had it out for you, but you didn't think she would go as far as to get you kicked out of school.

"But we didn't do anything wrong. So what makes her so sure?" you whisper to Willa. Willa is already half way inside the office where Dean Acheson is waving you in. She grabs your arm and jerks you in with her.

"Thank you both for coming. Is there anything either of you would like to say before we get started?" Dean Acheson asks as she sits across from you on the sofa and chairs set up in her office for more pleasant meetings like afternoon tea with visiting alumnae and parent conferences.

You and Willa exchange a puzzled look and shake your heads from side to side.

"Okay, then. Several of the residents of Moser Hall reported seeing you enter the building last night as they were leaving for dinner. And we have a source who tells us you were alone in the dorm," she says slowly looking directly at you.

Your blood runs cold and you freeze in your chair. So this is why Hayden was so cocky.

"I...we...went to Professor Carden's for dinner," you stammer.

"She invited us. We got permission from the Mitchells. You can ask them," Willa adds defensively.

"No, I'm aware of your reason for being there. That's not where my concern lies," she says softly. She has concern? Little alarm bells go off in your head. "Were you in fact alone in the dorm at any point during the night?"

"Well, yes. I mean, we were making a pie, and Samantha sent me to the kitchen to get a pie plate. One of her dorm girls had borrowed it," you explain calmly. And that was the truth.

"And how long did that take...roughly?" the Dean asks, taking little notes in a cloth-covered book. You stare at her pen, which stops waits for your answer.

"Um...maybe five or six minutes?" you say glancing at Willa for confirmation.

"Six minutes to get a pie plate?" the Dean parrots.

"Well, I've never been to Moser Hall before, and they keep things in different places than we do in our kitchen. I had to search through the cabinets," you explain, feeling like you are on the witness stand in a courtroom. But surely you can't be convicted for something you didn't even do.

"I see. And that's the only time you were alone in the dorm?" She glances down at the details in her detective journal. Willa flashes you a look of sympathy.

"Well, there was one other time," you say, the words sinking in your stomach like a stone thrown into a muddy pond. "We were dyeing Willa's hair, and Samantha spilled the peroxide all over the bathroom floor. I had to go down to the second floor to look for a mop in the utility closet."

"She was only gone for a few minutes!" Willa cries, trying to help.

"But you were alone," the Dean confirms looking directly into your eyes.

"Yes," you whisper. Everyone knows the second floor is where Claudia Everheart's room is, from which the earrings were stolen.

Dean Acheson turns her head and sizes you up from the side of her eye. "You know, I used to be a gymnast and my coach always said 'how quickly you get back on the beam matters more than the fact that you fell off in the first place'." You nod and smile. Willa looks even more confused. "We all make mistakes. It's how we correct them that matters. So there's nothing else you want to tell me?" the Dean repeats.

You want to tell her the saga of what's been happening to you and the theory that's taking shape in your head, but something tells you this isn't the right time. You don't have all the clues, so you keep your mouth shut.

"Okay girls," Dean Acheson says loudly as she stands up to adjourn your meeting. "Thank you for your cooperation. I'll let you know if I need anything else." She smiles at you and Willa but her eyes are locked with yours.

"That lockjaw, town and county brat is trying to say I stole those earrings," you say once you and Willa are well out of earshot of the Dean or anyone for that matter.

"I told you. Even Carden thought she was behind it. But how do we prove it?" she wonders.

"I don't know yet. But it all makes sense. She's wanted to get back at me since I booted her out of my room that first day. And I ran into her in Moser Hall last night. Didn't you hear what she said to me going into the Dean's office? She has to be their 'source.'"

"Plus, don't forget the time Anupa was helping you with your vanishing assignment and she found that pink marabou feather in your room. Maybe Hayden's been stealing the jewelry all along. Now she wants to frame you for it. I don't know. It sounds crazy, she's so cream cheese perfect, it would almost make sense. We need to talk to Carden. She'll know what to do. Plus, she can vouch for us...ur... you," Willa says. And she's right. Your heart flutters with relief. This does make more sense. You knew Samantha was on your side. You still don't know what that shimmer was about, but why would Samantha be out to get you? It just doesn't add up. Hayden is petty, competitive, and vindictive. Samantha has done nothing but be your friend. You decide to take your chances and go see Samantha after lunch.

You spend your entire French class watching the minute hand on the clock that hangs above Madame Baldur's desk. Seventy-five clicks that drop into your ears and join the river of sound flowing through your head. You'll have to get notes from someone tomorrow because you haven't heard a word of her lesson. All you can think about is Hayden Murdoch and her campaign of cruelty. The more you think about it, the more certain you are that she is the one who's been wrecking your life.

The only detail that still doesn't fit is the intercepted invitation to join The Field, which happened before you ever met her. You'll have to wait to see the big picture before you can piece it together with the other events. But all you know is the villain is not Samantha. And that's really all that matters. When the clock strikes four o'clock, you leap from your seat and charge out of the room. Samantha keeps office hours from 4:00-6:00, and you want to be the first one to get there.

You walk so quickly and with such purpose towards the rectangular building on the other side of the student center, the leaves behind you swirl up in your wake. You cut behind the rotunda to avoid the crowds of girls meeting up after class to nibble on nuggets of news they've collected and jovial teammates heading to practice.

"Hey!" someone shouts and you glance behind you, but your feet don't stop moving. You wouldn't pause for the President right now. Anupa jogs to catch up and tries to keep pace, which isn't hard. Her legs are about five inches longer than yours, and she's fueled by adrenaline from the high-tech coup she has just pulled off.

"Guess what?!" she says, grabbing your arm. You've never seen her so lit up. "I finally got into Blackboard! You should've seen it – they had everything from firewalls to filters to passwords to hijackware. It was like a virtual Fort Knox, and I was a secret agent swooping through back door booby traps and –"

"Anupa!" you didn't have time for her cyber-high babble. You feel the tears starting to form in your eyes. "I think Hayden's behind it all and now she's somehow trying to get me kicked out," you blurt out way too loudly. Her excitement is contagious.

Anupa stops in her tracks and yanks you to a stop with her. "Really? But I traced your Greek translation to someone in town. It's a local account that went through a local server."

"Hayden sneaks into town all the time with Erica and Danielle," you snip.

Anupa looks skeptical. "But this would take a pretty internet-savvy person. They had to bypass a lot of the school's online security too. Are you sure Little Miss Congeniality is capable of that?"

"Probably not. But she's got unlimited money. I'm sure she

just paid someone to do it for her. Listen, I've got go talk to Samantha. I really appreciate your efforts. I'll catch up with you later, okay?" you say over your shoulder as you start off. You feel a pang of guilt just marching off, but you don't have any time to waste.

When you arrive at Samantha's you are relieved to see her door open, which means she's not meeting with a student or on the phone. Peeking in, you see her standing in front of an avant-garde painting projected on the wall by a small machine in the corner. She looks like a painting herself, in a ruffled collar blouse and high-waisted, bell-cuff pants. Classical music plays softly from little speakers on her desk.

"Hey," you say as you knock lightly on the door frame.

She spins around and smiles, "Hey you!" she nods cheerily, closing her notebook and giving you a squeeze. Your face flushes with a mixture of shame and affection. How could you ever have suspected her or had such dark thoughts? That stupid shimmer was just a mirage, probably nothing. This is the real Samantha, your fellow foster survivor and friend. The one who shows you everyday that anything is possible.

"Sorry, I hope I'm not interrupting anything important."

"Oh, no. I was just writing my lecture for Thursday's seminar. What's up?" She plops down at her desk and takes a drink from a mug of tea that's been steeping.

You close the door and sit down across from her. You're surprisingly cool-headed considering what you're about to reveal. "I need your help."

"Of course," she says without hesitation.

"You were right about Hayden. She must've been the one in my room. But that's not all. I saw her coming out of the Dean's office right before I got called in and grilled about the missing earrings. They know I was in Moser Hall, and it sounds like they think I stole them! She must be trying to frame me or something!"

Her eyes bulge in disbelief.

"Oh my god! She's out of control."

"I know," you agree. You're glad she's as outraged as you are. "I need you to talk to the Dean for me. I think they think I stole the earrings when I was alone in the dorm getting the pie plate or the mop. I don't know what Hayden told them but the Dean was acting really weird. Like she was trying to get me to confess or something. Have they talked to you yet?"

"Not yet, but I've been teaching all day. Listen, Hayden is a real piece of work. She's notorious among the faculty and staff. But I'll talk to the Dean and see what I can find out. If nothing else…"

As Samantha speaks, she takes a sip from her mug and, for the first time, you notice what is written on it in bold green letters: "Come See What You're Missing in Watch Hill, Rhode Island!" The symphony in your head hits a resounding crescendo and your mouth goes dry. "…I can reassure them that you weren't gone long. I mean, I can't say you were with me the whole time, but it should help put their minds at ease." She glances at the clock. "My office hours go to six, and then I just have to run to…do an errand in town. But I'll find the Dean as soon as I get back," she says smiling over the rim of her cup.

She had confided in Willa about the house she keeps in town – is that where she's going? At the time, you were envious she trusted Willa enough to keep her juicy little secret for her. But now that chunk of information is rotting in your brain and you can't ignore the stench of suspicion it gives off after what Anupa just told you.

"Where did you get that cup?" you ask, trying to sound casual.

She holds out the mug and looks at it fondly. "Oh, this? I was house-sitting for a friend over the summer. Watch Hill is a little beach town, it's sort of near Mystic. She just sent this to me as a gag thank you gift. Isn't it sublimely touristy and banal? She's a riot."

You instantly flash to the shimmer you had of Samantha on the porch of a beach house. You've never shimmered the past, so you thought you were seeing her on some future break or holiday. But this is what the shimmer was trying to show you, that she was the one who hijacked your online account. While she spent the summer helping her friend, she ensured you wouldn't have a single one at your new school.

You're body begins to tremble. Giant cymbals clash together inside your head as your heart jumps into your throat.

"You were in Watch Hill this summer?" you croak over the percussion explosion. It feels like the air is being sucked out of the room along with everything you thought you had figured out. You look around wildly waiting for the walls to implode. You want to get up and run but your knees are so weak, you're afraid your legs will fold in half with no hinge to hold them together.

"Yeah, why? What's wrong?" she asks looking at you strangely. "Are you okay? You look really pale all of a sudden," she says, alarm registering in her voice.

Before you know it you're on your feet. Your heart is beating so fast before you've even taken a step. You need to get out of here now. You need your friends, your real friends, to help you. You tug on the door and fling it open, running down the empty hall and refusing to look back or answer Samantha's calls to return. If someone was watching, you're sure they wouldn't see your feet touch the ground. You have to find Anupa. Now! So you head to the one place you know you can always find her.

"Anupa!" you say, barging into the room. She's in the middle of tutoring a group of Third Formers about the pitfalls of pop-ups and phishing and spyware. But when she sees your tear-streaked face, she knows it can't wait. She excuses herself and takes you into a small storage room full of back-up hard drives and boxes.

"You look like you've seen a ghost!" Anupa says as she pats your back.

"More like a Trojan Horse," you choke.

"Girlfriend, calm down. Take a deep breath," Anupa says, waiting for you to recover. "I have news that might make you feel better. I was able to find the physical address of the house in town from where your paper was ripped off."

"Good. 'Cause I just found out that Samantha spent the summer in Watch Hill, Rhode Island," you sputter resting your head against the wall. You can tell from Anupa's face she gets the significance.

"I knew this whole thing was bigger than Hayden! That pretentious, glamorized guppy. Samantha's the kind of big fish that could pull off something like that. I've chatted with her online, she knows her stuff when it comes to web design and servers, and all of that. And as a professor, she would have authorization on Blackboard and your account information. It would be a snap."

"I bet that address you found is her secret apartment in town," you say.

"She has a secret apartment in town?" Anupa cries. "Is she like some double agent or just a total psycho?"

"Hard to tell at this point," you reply seriously.

"And what the hell did you ever do to her?"

"I don't know. But she's not done. I have a feeling she's gonna do something tonight. I have to go to that house," you say soberly.

"Okay, now you've lost it. Is her psychosis contagious?" she asks, taking a step back and shaking her head. "You can't go there."

You desperately want to tell Anupa about your shimmers so she'll understand that you know you have to expose Samantha before she gets you expelled. But you don't know how to say it.

"Anupa, I'll explain later. Just trust me on this one. I know what I know," you say looking into her worried eyes.

She bites her lip as she considers. "Okay. But only if I go with you."

"Anupa, no!" you insist. She's already helped you enough by hacking into the system several times.

"But I'm the only one who can get into her computer, if it's there. And we'll need your paper as hard evidence if we want to bust her!"

The girl has a point.

"Okay, if you're sure. Thank you Anupa!" you throw your arms around her neck. "But what about your class in there?" you ask, both of you peeking through the crack in the door.

"This is way more important," she says dismissively. She steps out and tells the wide-eyed girls they're done for the day. You and she run all the way back to Rose House to find Casey and Willa. You're going to need their help to pull this off.

Casey and Willa are rocked when you fill them in on your discoveries and what you plan to do that night.

"I can't believe Samantha would do this to you. I thought she was our friend," Willa marvels.

"I can," Casey says grimly. The three of you stare at her in shock.

"What do you mean?" you, Willa, and Anupa say in unison, a choir of disbelief.

She runs out of the room and returns moments later with two pieces of paper in her hands. "That's what I was trying to tell you last night. I was in your room borrowing your Sacred Texts book when I noticed these two notes pinned on your bulletin board," she says holding out your soccer note and the M&M invitation. "Check out the similarity in the handwriting!" The three of you lean in to examine them closer. "Look how the 'r' is curled on the end and the way the 'I' slants, and the shape of her a's — they're exactly the same."

"Why didn't you show me this last night?" you cry.

"I was going to but you looked so sick. Plus, I knew Samantha is important to you. What was I supposed to say 'hey, sorry you're sick, but I just wanted to tell you your mentor and friend screwed you over'? And what if I'd been wrong?" she says, her eyes filling with guilty tears.

"Casey! It's okay. You were just being a good friend," you say, patting her shoulder. She sniffles, and the tears begin to absorb back into her big brown eyes. But you can tell she is still hanging on to something. You could drive a dump truck down the ditches worry lines are making in her forehead. She looks back at you and whimpers.

"Now what?" Anupa asks in exasperation.

"Skipping dinner service? Sneaking off campus? Breaking and entering into a professor's house? I don't even want to think about how many rules you'll be breaking." Casey's voice sounds breakable itself, and the tears swell again.

"How many we'll be breaking," Anupa corrects her. "C'mon guys, I know this is all hard to believe and our strategy sounds scary, but we can't do this without you."

Willa takes one look at your pleading faces and bounces back from bewilderment. "You're right. Samantha can't get away with this or you'll be gone. And I'm not gonna sit by and let that happen. I'm in," she says, rising to her feet. Her impish body flexes with ire as she rubs her hands together to prepare for battle.

Casey doesn't know how to not play by the rules, but the thought of losing you makes her want to break down for real. She doesn't click well with most girls, but it was different with you, and she knows that's worth saving. Even if it means not being so goodie goodie for one night.

"I'll help too," she says joining the circle the three of you have formed. You look around the group at each of their faces and you're filled with love and gratitude for your friends. This is your family. The one you've been looking for. You may not be linked by blood or genes but this bond is a choice, an act of love, and it's just as strong, if not stronger.

One hour later, you're sitting with Willa and Casey anxiously eyeing the main door to the dining hall. Anupa told the Mitchells she had a special tutoring session and got permission to eat dinner in the computer lab.

"Okay, let's go over this one more time," you say, just as much for your benefit as either of theirs. "When Samantha walks through that door, I'm gonna slip out to meet Anupa and Bailey. While he drives us to her love nest, the two of you are going to watch Samantha. Let her eat but then keep her here as long as you can. Willa, distract her with art history questions, whatever it takes. If she leaves, follow her to her apartment and stall her there. We need at least two hours to get there, do our thing, and get back. Got it?" They nod sternly. Casey chews nervously on her straw.

"I wish cell phones got reception around here!" Willa laments.

"I know," you whine. But at that moment, Samantha steps through the door and the three of you exchange a knowing look. "It's go time," you whisper and slide off your chair.

You carry your tray to the rows of trashcans and glance around the room to make sure no one is watching. You rush past them and duck behind a divider wall into the kitchen. You dodge a cook with watery eyes from chopping onions. He stares at you blankly, surprised to see a student on his turf. But as quickly as you appeared, you escape through a side door marked "staff only."

You dash across campus to the back edge of the skeet fields where the visitor parking lot is. That's where Anupa is waiting for you with Bailey in his car. They are in the last space of the lot with the headlights turned off. Thank God it's a Prius so the silent engine can stay running.

"Thanks Bailey. I owe you one," you say as you climb into the front seat. Anupa was brilliant to think of him when you were trying to figure out how to get into town. Harrowgate is too small to have taxicabs and the two of you riding your bikes down the main road into town would've been too obvious and taken too long.

"Nah. Anupa's got you covered. She already ordered a top-of-the-line thermal cooler for my Pentium chip," he says eagerly. You have no idea what he's talking about but based on his ear-to-ear grin, you know it means something in his world. You also know he would've done this favor for free, and gladly be fired from his job as the Tech Guru of TW, to have Anupa Lahiri in his car.

You pull up to a small bungalow situated next to a crystal-clear stream. Bailey pulls around back where there's a small patio with a mostly glass door. "I'll stay right here," Bailey says reassuringly. "I can see almost the entire yard from here. If I see anyone or anything weird, I'll flash my lights." You and Anupa nod and climb out.

You use a blanket from Bailey's trunk to muffle the sound as you break the glass on the door with a rock. "I saw it in a movie once," you say to Anupa, who raises her charcoal eyebrows to show she's impressed. The two of you flip on your flashlights and creep inside. You lead the way down a narrow hallway that opens up into a cavernous living room. You immediately recognize the room and its mammoth fireplace, blackened with ashes from recent use, from your shimmer. The high-back chair you envisioned is next to the window with a rotary phone and a glazed table nearby.

"This is it. This is her place," you say out loud. And the sound of rushing water fills the space around you.

"Yup, this is her desktop alright," Anupa confirms. Her voice sounds smaller, like she's moved far away. You spin around, suddenly frightened of being alone. She's sitting behind a desk with a new desktop Mac on top of it in a small archway nook made into an office.

"Bingo," she says as her fingers rapidly tap the keys. "She didn't even have a password. Amateur," she snarks.

While she works quickly, you stand in the middle of the room. You know you should be rifling shelves and snooping through drawers, but instead you just stare at the eye candy all around you – books, photos, mementos. A stack of fashion magazines lies haphazardly in a basket by the chair. Part of you doesn't want to find anything else. You'd prefer to write off Samantha as a sociopath who randomly chose you as her target. Anything more personal or unusual may mean this is bigger than the irrational animosity of a nut job professor. What if you find something that ties her to all that stuff Elizabeth Wilmington was talking about? Or worse, proves she lied about being a foster kid? You won't let your brain go there, not now.

You wander into the bedroom, the only other room beside the kitchen. There's only enough space for a small bed and a storage trunk at the end. You open the lid and stare down at the contents. A few cashmere sweaters folded and stacked in one corner, a blanket, a parka, and two thick scarves take up the rest of the hollow box. Just as you are closing the top, a bright flash of red catches your eye. You reach in and pull out a wadded up handkerchief from between the sweaters. Inside you make a stunning discovery – the gold daisy necklace with diamonds in the center of each little flower. It's just like the one that the mousy girl described! There's also a pair or diamond hoops, a large ring with a pear shaped emerald in the middle, and a black leather cuff with a jewel encrusted hinge. "Jackpot," you say to yourself. So this was how Samantha was planning to bring you down. She's probably planted the other pieces somewhere in your room.

Suddenly, the room lights up as if it were daytime. Your head whips up, your heart pounds. Then you are in the darkness again. The room lights up again. It's Bailey. That's his SOS signal for trouble.

"Anupa?!" you shout shoving the jewelry in your pocket and closing the trunk.

Thud! You collide with Anupa in the darkened hallway. She holds up a CD as she rubs her head vigorously. "I got it! Your paper was on her hard drive. I have everything we need backed up right here," she waves it giddily and hops up and down. "Ow," the sudden jolts makes her head throb harder.

"I found some of the pieces of stolen jewelry!" you gasp. "But we gotta get out of here. Bailey flashed his lights." Suddenly, you hear a jingling of keys and the rusted deadbolt on the front door begin to turn. "OH MY GOD! It's Samantha!" You grab Anupa's hand and silently sprint out the back door.

"That was close!" Bailey says as you tumble into the car. "I saw Professor Carden pull up while you guys were in there. I flashed my lights, but when you didn't come out right away, I thought we were toast!"

"Just get us out of here!" you say as he speeds off.

The rest of the car ride back to school is spent in silence. The gentle rhythm of the tires on the old country road soothes your frazzled nerves. The protective adrenaline leaches from your body and your energy trickles out with it. Anupa sits in the back staring out the window while Bailey gazes at her from the rearview mirror. When you pull up into the visitor parking lot, Willa and Casey are waiting for you, pacing like cats along the curb.

"Oh thank god!" Casey exclaims as they run up to meet the car. Bailey drops you off and then bolts. He's risked enough for one night. Casey bowls you over with a hug and then turns on Anupa with the same overpowering affection. "We tried to keep Samantha distracted as long as we could, but she was mega agitated. It's like she knew why we were there." The words are toppling out of Casey's mouth faster than she can move her lips; a few words clump together and fall out in big blocks of sound.

"You should've seen her, she couldn't even sit still for five seconds. When we went with her to her apartment, that's when she knew something was up. She got a phone call and rushed out saying she had to meet her boyfriend in town," Willa adds as the four of you head to Rose House to organize evidence and prepare for the final phase of the plan – turning Samantha in and clearing your name once and for all.

"We know. She showed up at the house!" Anupa announces triumphantly.

"While you were still there? Did she see you?" Casey screeches.

"Nope. We snuck out the back. But just barely!" The jeopardy and excitement are bonding them thick as thieves. "But not before I got the paper off her computer and copied a few other files that looked interesting. Samantha's about to get trapped like the rat that she is," Anupa says smugly.

"Being bad is kind of fun!" Casey blurts out to the group as you run in a herd. You all look at each other and dissolve into giggles.

Casey's night of being bad has left its mark. It feels good to laugh out loud after such an intense night. For just a moment, things feel normal again. As you cross the threshold to your dorm, you're reminded again of what great friends you have and how lucky you are, even in the midst of all this craziness.

But when you arrive at your suite, it's no laughing matter. Headmistress Cadwell, Dean Acheson, the Mitchells, and campus security are waiting for you in the common room.

"Please come inside girls, and take a seat," Madame Cadwell says with such authority, the four of you shuffle in obediently and squeeze onto the sofa without saying a word.

"I'm afraid we have a very serious situation that deserves everyone's immediate attention and requires everyone's absolute honesty." You can see the sick green worry swirling around in the black pools of her eyes, but she remains poised – shoulders back, hands clasped in front, a pillar of assertiveness. "As you know, we've been gravely concerned about the recent thefts on campus. I care deeply for each girl here as if she were my own." She looks straight at you. "That is why it pains me so to say... we received an anonymous tip this evening and found this in your sports locker."

Dean Acheson holds up the missing sapphire bracelet. It glints in the light reflecting your guilt for everyone to see. "And these were between the cushions of that very couch," the Dean frowns. She uncurls her hand to reveal two huge diamond rocks on gold posts.

So that's what Samantha was doing prowling around your suite last night. You glance down the row, expecting to see the blood-drained faces of your friends staring back, but instead they are feverish, a line of thoroughbreds lined up at the gate chomping at the bit and on a mouth full of information. Willa is actually sitting on her hands to keep from waving them wildly in the air to interrupt.

"Madame Cadwell, I know this looks bad, but I can explain," you say hurriedly.

"No need for that," the guard says as he leans over and pulls on the tail end of the diamond daisy necklace that's sticking out of your pocket. "You've been caught red-handed," he swags as he hands it over to the Dean. It sounds like an old black-and-white detective show with bad actors and even worse writing. But no, it's happening, live and in color in your common room.

"Samantha Carden is the thief. She's been the one stealing all along and she planted that jewelry to get me kicked out. It's part of some elaborate crusade she's carrying out against me!" you tell them. You are on your feet, but you don't remember standing up. Lily and the Dean gasp right on cue. The security guard and Gordon both knit their brows in doubt. But Madame Cadwell stays very still and quiet.

"That is a very serious accusation, young lady. I hope you have some kind of proof to back it up," Gordon states. That's when your friends leap into action. Weeks of wind sprints for JV soccer have made Casey's legs swift and powerful. She's off the couch like a shot; she darts to her room and back before the security guard can take a step towards the hall. She's completely consumed by her bold, new bad-girl persona. With her chin flipped up, eyes squinting in triumph, and her right hand on her jutted out hip, she hands over the two notes with great satisfaction.

"Both of these notes were written by Professor Carden. The handwriting is identical. Samantha planted a fake note in her mailbox so she would miss the scrimmage. And that's exactly what happened. Sabotage. She got in trouble with Coach Carlson, her teammates were furious, she had to stuff envelopes all day and missed the trip to Boston," Casey says all in one breath. Madame Cadwell takes the notes and compares the writing. The Mitchells stoop to read over her shoulder. Lily is clutching her chest, tight with concern.

Anupa spins the silver CD-ROM on her index finger. It's her moment to shine. "And this has the computer codes and commands that proves Samantha stole her Greek translation from Blackboard and deleted it from her laptop, lickety split. She had a copy of the paper on her desktop, along with some other files you're going to want to look at. She's got a ledger that would make Donald Trump jealous. And there's a list of women with some extremely prominent names," Anupa says as she hands over the CD. She sends a wink in Casey's direction who gives her a friendly nod of approval.

You pull out the other ring and hoop earrings you found in Samantha's trunk. "These were stashed with the daisy necklace. I don't know if they're hers or if they're also stolen, but I didn't have a lot of time to decide. You guys can see to it they're returned to their rightful owner," you say gently laying the pieces onto the coffee table.

"And don't forget, Samantha blocked all of her Field invites over the summer from her friend's home in Watch Hill, " Willa adds, thrilled to serve up her own slice of proof pie. "That's why she never knew about the site or posted anything about herself. Samantha saw to it that she was kept in the dark. Can you imagine how she must've felt knowing everyone else had been chatting and making friends all summer?" Willa cries.

And she is literally about to cry – her eyes turn glassy with hot tears of frustration. It occurs to you for the first time that Willa was betrayed by Samantha too. She looked up to her as a mentor and trusted her as a friend. And now she cries for you, for herself, and for the universe at large because she knows what you all have lost because of what Samantha has done. Willa told you once that she believes that "all human beings are one; their souls come from the same source. Like a beam of light fractured into millions of radiant slivers."

And, because of that, she knows people are meant to treat each other with kindness and love. Willa is the real deal. And every time someone was more "human" than "being," it hurts right down to her soul.

Madame Cadwell turns to Anupa. "Is that true? Do you have evidence of that online piracy as well?"

Anupa nods earnestly. The Dean and the Headmistress exchange a distressed look. "This is all very hard to believe..." Madame Cadwell finally says.

"We can take you to her apartment in town and show you in person if you'd like," you say quickly. "I don't know if she's still there, but either way –"

"She has an apartment in town?" all of the adults say at once, their voices blending together in a single phrase.

"Yeah, can you believe her?" Casey shouts. She's really out of her shell.

"But she never told us that. Professors are supposed to disclose all personal facts – residences, family, significant others," the Dean says shaking her head. "Not to mention, we do extensive background checks on everyone who steps foot on this campus. How did she manage to hide that from us?" she wonders out loud.

"We better go there now," the security guard chimes in. "If she was there when you were leaving, she may have already gotten away."

You have to bite your lip to keep from snickering. Everything he says sounds like cheesy cop dialogue, but the man's right. The 'who' and the 'how' may have been revealed, but there is one more question burns red hot on the tip of your tongue. Why? And you can't wait to look Samantha Carden in the eyes and ask her that very question.

But things rarely happen in life in the exact way and at the exact time you want them to.

When you arrive at her apartment, Samantha is nowhere in sight. There is evidence of her panicked preparations for her get-away everywhere you look. No need for your flashlight this time, every light in the house is flipped on, and the front and back doors remain wide open. Her clothing is flung all over her tiny bedroom, and one of her suitcases sits face up and half-packed on her bed. Every drawer and cabinet is ajar, their contents dumped onto the floor and strewn along the counters. Dean Acheson finds a list of locker combinations in a pile of torn papers, and you come across a stack of TW stationary scattered by the bookshelf in the corner of the living room. The trusty security guard turns up a cell phone in the gravel driveway.

"She must've accidentally dropped it while loading up her car," he surmises. "One of the sent calls is to the Headmistress's office. That's your 'anonymous tip,'" he concludes confidently.

But she didn't take much. Just her computer and some clothes, as though she'll be taken care of wherever she's going or can simply buy a whole new McLife as soon as she feels peckish for a job and some friends and a home. Something tells you she won't just recede into the shadows for a quiet life on the lam.

The next morning, Madame Cadwell calls the four of you into her office. She sits you down and makes you hold hands. It's strange to see a woman like Edith Cadwell sitting on the floor, her stockinged legs tucked under her knit skirt – a stunning swan seated on the algae green carpet. She belongs on a stage, on a dais, or behind a podium. But being outside her natural habitat doesn't detract from her dignified aesthetic. "I know this has been a very traumatic couple of days, or even weeks, for all of you. While I wish you had come to me sooner, I commend you for your bravery, maturity, and deductive reasoning in this whole matter. You've taken on a bigger burden at your young age than some people do their entire lives. And you've done this school a tremendous service."

This whole time you had been so focused on what was happening to you, you had not considered what else a person like Samantha had up her sleeve for other girls or the school in general.

"But I must ask one more favor of each of you. Can I depend on you to not speak of this matter until we can investigate Miss Carden and this whole incident? I know it's a lot to ask, but it is the only way to ensure we get to the bottom of this without unnecessary rumors or permanent damage to our community."

There is something about the light in her eyes and the circuit of energy coursing around the circle of your hands that makes you all understand how important this is. Of course you'll turn over the Rubik's cube of memories in your head trying to make the facts line up and your feelings make sense. And you'll probably talk about it amongst yourselves, at least for a while, until the scab falls off and there's nothing else to pick. Gossip and rumors and the exchange of secrets are only human nature. By the time you turn 14, everyone has promised to guard a secret for a friend or agreed not to blab in exchange for a deliciously dirty scoop on someone they know. Some news is just too good to hold onto and you have to run and tell. But not this. You can hear each other's hearts beat and you nod your heads to the collective tempo. Your promise to Madame Cadwell may as well be tattooed on your skin because it is a part of you now, and if you double-crossed her you'd really be hurting yourself.

At the Assembly on Friday morning, the Dean announces that Professor Carden had to go on leave indefinitely due to a personal matter. This was not entirely unbelievable. The distinguished professors that Trumbull Woodhouse attracts often take sabbaticals to write a book or get married or travel for extensive research on a thesis they are developing. TW even grants some paid leaves to long-standing employees. But any departure is decided well in advance so the class schedule can be planned around it. And so students can bring flowers and send their heartfelt wishes during lingering goodbyes. Professors never leave unannounced or in the middle of the semester.

"Professor Takahito, who taught Art History at Mount Holyoke College before being hired by Trumbull, will take over those classes. And Assistant Field Hockey Coach Lannan will be assume the Coach position. It will be a seamless transition, and anyone who has any difficulty can come directly to me," the Dean instructs. The announcement leaves the student body shocked, especially the girls who work with Samantha every day. They feel like she took a piece of them with her. That night there are more headaches and stomachaches and girls asking for aspirin than usual.

"Those girls don't know how lucky they are," Anupa says as she passes by the nurse's office. Diagnosis: Samantha Withdrawl, their charts should read. "They miss the woman they thought she was. If only they knew the truth."

The truth is that the truth is ugly and scary. The truth would make their stomachs cramp with anxiety if it was fed to them instead of the sugar water version the Dean spooned out. Granted, these girls know how cruel adults can be to each other in the name of power, money, envy, or spite. They've sat on stairwells listening to their mothers discover affairs and divorce; they've been in courtrooms for custody hearings and alimony suits. They've even seen their family's name maligned on society pages and run through the mud of the tabloids. But it would sicken them to see the same wickedness and ruthlessness carried out on kids. Their lips and ears would turn black and their eyes would see spots if they knew Samantha had been as sadistic as she was. But the funny thing is, you and your friends have been living with the real story for the past few days, the dark truth and all of Samantha's devious acts, and you've never felt better.

You step out of Rose House and tilt your face up to the vanilla sky. It snowed last night for the first time. You stayed up late watching the flurries of fresh snowflakes fall in the darkness. When you woke up and wiped the frost from the window, the campus had been transformed by a dusting of snow. The dorms and cottages have white gutter moustaches and the giant black dome of the student center looks like it's been draped with Hayden's duvet. The snow cleanses everything and makes it seem pure, as if this thin layer of frozen water has washed away whatever came before and whatever lies underneath.

You take a deep breath and open your eyes. One by one the girls are emerging from their dorms. It's Saturday morning, and there are meals to eat, homework to complete, supplies to buy, journals to update, books to read, gossip to spread, and sports to play. As you pass the little gazebo where Fifth Formers sneak cigarettes and the entrance to the Rose Garden, Elizabeth's house comes into view. Maybe it's the sight of her glowworm cottage, maybe it's the infectious joy from the girls' whoops and cheers that echo in your ears, maybe it's simply the rich blood spreading through your veins from a brisk walk in the cold. But in that moment you are filled with the sense that everything is different and yet nothing has changed.

The events with Samantha came to a head so quickly, you didn't have time to go to Elizabeth for help or even advice. You weren't surprised to find another winsome invitation, printed in fairytale cursive on her signature blue paper, in your mailbox Friday morning. You're not sure how she will react to the events of the past week, and you can't decide if you want to know more about the mystical history of the school.

When you arrive, there is a note on the door to let yourself in, and you step into her cloistered entryway. You remove your coat, scarf, gloves, and hat, hanging them on the coat rack by the door. The bittersweet voice of a female soprano floats softly through the living room from invisible speakers, and an intoxicating mixture of smells wafts from the kitchen. Pumpkin, cinnamon, vanilla, and brown sugar seeps from the walls, but you don't hear the clink of silverware, pans or dishes.

"Elizabeth? I'm here," you call out, not wanting to startle her.

You pass through the kitchen, the cats batting playfully at your feet, and come upon Elizabeth setting the table on her glassed-in patio. Clusters of votives flicker, casting a champagne incandescence on her face and magnificent white hair. Through the glass walls you can see her icy yard and frost-tipped trees. A row of snow sits atop the short picket fence that outlines the borders of her gardens. Little sticks, naming each kind of vegetable and flower, poke out like candles on a lightly frosted cake. Against this backdrop she turns and smiles, a lion peering at you from the wintry woods.

"I'm so glad to see you," she says with such sincerity that you let out a little whimper. "My little soldier." She wraps her arms around you, the deep purple sleeves of her dress enveloping your face and neck. You breathe in her sweet rose perfume.

"You've been to battle and back as I understand it," she says as you both take your seats. For the first time you feel like you've earned a place at her table. She's apologetic, but doesn't seem the least bit surprised or alarmed by your adventure. "I didn't realize how desperate they are or the lengths they will go to in order to maintain their positions of wealth and power," she says, shaking her head. "They must think you are The One."

"I'm sorry to interrupt, but who are 'they?' Are we talking about more than just Professor Carden?" you ask, trying to swallow the bite of banana-nut waffle you have in your mouth. You have a feeling her answer will take care of your appetite.

Elizabeth sighs and stares at you. Her dark eyes make it hard to look anywhere else, but in your peripheral vision you notice she has not touched her plate. And her knuckles are white where her hand grips the fork, She places it down on the mosaic tile table and folds her palms under her chin. She opens and closes her mouth several times before saying anything, as if the words she wants need coaxing to come out from deep in her throat.

"My dear, there's more to the story I was telling you about during our last visit," she begins. "Much more."

An uneasy feeling creeps up your spine, causing you to sit up straighter in your seat. You instinctively scoot your chair closer and, almost crush the paw of the cat that is curled around the base of your chair.

"I didn't want to discuss this until you were ready, but I see now that in my attempt to shelter you from the onus this information carries, I only weakened your ability to protect yourself. And you do need protecting. Do you remember the society of women I told you about? The women charged with guiding girls with special abilities?"

You nod and try to swallow, but your throat is too dry. You just gulp in air that sticks in your chest and aches like it does every time you think about your shimmers.

"Emma Woodhouse was one herself. She had extraordinary abilities; some called them 'powers.' She could into someone's eyes and tell what they were thinking. She could feel people's presences even when they were states away. But her greatest gift, her strongest power, was the visions she had of the future."

It's a good thing your legs are securely tucked under the table, which is weighted down with food and dishes. Or you would rocket right out of your seat, ricochet off the walls like a bolt of lightning, and land on the floor in a bewildered lump. And it's a good thing Elizabeth keeps talking or you would swear you had imagined what she just said.

"Emma had her first vision when she was a young girl, about your same age, visiting her grandfather's farm for the summer. His farm became this very campus. In a clearing here, there is a spring that we call the Source. It is a reservoir of power that flows from the core of the universe itself. She went to this magical meadow to write all of her visions in a book called The Apocrophyn. No one knows why, but the ink fades over time if it is not properly...rejuvenated... with eleven drops from the Source each year."

Elizabeth narrows her eyes, and you have to shift in your seat to keep from sinking into the floor. "Members of our society are the only ones who knew of its existence and the astoundingly accurate predictions The Apocryphon contains. Years ago, the members of the society came from all over the world to hold a meeting on campus and visit the Source to perform the water ceremony. At all other times, The Apocrophyn was kept in a secret crypt under the center altar in the Chapel."

"Sorry, but you keep using the past tense. Don't you do those things anymore?" you ask, trying to keep up.

Elizabeth clears her throat. "The Apocryphon disappeared shortly after the schism formed among the leaders of the Secret Society almost 30 years ago." She shudders despite the warmth of the room. "You see, I believe the splinter faction has been using The Apocryphon to make investments for their own gain, under the guises of investing for the school endowment. Over the years they strategically planted members on the Finance Committee in an effort to hide their schemes."

Without thinking, you let out a light whistle under your breath. Elizabeth stifles a smile. "From the little I've seen of this school so far, I can only imagine how much money that is," you say candidly.

"Trust me, even the wealthiest men in the world would find it impressive. That's the problem, that kind of money in the wrong hands, funding the wrong causes, subsidizing people like

Samantha Carden... you can see why we're worried. Not to mention, they are indiscriminate in their choice of investments. All they care about is making more money, even if it means benefitting from others' suffering."

"What do you mean, like stocks and stuff?" you say naively.

"Yes, but even bigger. Emma's predictions include worldwide events like the increasing seismic and geomantic activity in the Gulf and the resulting devastation to New Orleans during Katrina. The Trumbull endowment trustees placed extraordinary bets on oil and gas futures months before the storm hit. It was so out of the blue, the futures dealers thought they were crazy, and collecting would be like taking candy from a baby. But the trustees made several hundred million dollars off that tragic event."

"A hundred million dollars?" you blurt out. "Does that much money even exist?!"

"A few times over," she says softly, finding your wide-eyed incredulity endearing. "I'm afraid that's where you come in," she says straightening her placemat and refolding her napkin. At first you think she's was just being compulsively tidy, but then her words filter into your brain. And you realize she's being kind and giving you a moment to freak out.

"Me?" you say. Your voice echoes and sounds far away. You place one hand on the side of your head just in case it decides to pop off.

She stops her busywork and reaches across the table, grasping your hand. Your skin sizzles from electric shock of her powerful touch.

"They think you're the one Emma Woodhouse predicted – The One who will come and reclaim The Apocryphon, the endowment, and reunite the Society once and for all. She said it would be an orphan and she would have more natural power than all of the Society members combined."

"Me?" is all you can manage to say again.

"You're one of the special ones we've been watching for awhile. It's no accident you're here."

You can't breathe, and the room is starting to go dark. "Do they...you... know about my shimmers?" you hear yourself say. But it sounds garbled like you're talking underwater, or through a tin can. The familiar tingling and heat that you've felt all you life now surges through your body and the darkness spreads.

"Yes," are the last words you hear her say.

A cacophony of shimmers rocks you to your core.

You're in a meadow. There's a pond with crystal clear water, and a thick muddy bank speckled with blooming white flowers. You've seen this before. Women's voices, low and deep, chanti-ng.

A gust of wind dissolves the scene to the amber colored tabletop where you can see your glittering name written in an ancient book. It's crossed through with blood red ink on a burning page. Drops of water fall and singe the flames.

Ruby liquid, the color of blood, obscures your view and covers your mind's eye. You can barely make out Samantha's smiling face, your acceptance letter to Trumbull Woodhouse, the strange woman's face on the airplane.

Then the red sea subsides and you're back in the meadow. It's quiet and serene. The breeze sways the vines hanging over the water.

Suddenly, your real senses are zapped back to life. The brick floor of the patio comes rushing back. The colors on Elizabeth's dress are more vibrant and clear than ever. She is standing over you holding two pale green cubes under your nose. She cups them in her hand and returns them to a secret pocket hidden deep in the folds of the fabric of her dress.

"There. That's better." she soothes.

"I think I've seen the Source. Just now. And before. It was a shimmer I had at my thirteenth birthday."

"The one that started you on your journey here," she says knowingly, as if this is a sign. Maybe it's something Emma Woodhouse wrote in her book.

"But there were others there. And all that blood. . . ." She stands you up and helps you to your chair. "Something's about to happen. Something important in that meadow but I can't tell if it's good or bad," you report. You don't know why you suddenly feel like crying.

"There's no need to worry for now, my dear. I've placed a protective spell on the Source, so it's safe for the moment. But the more time that passes, the weaker the spell gets. The Source and The Apocryphon, for that matter."

The phone rings from inside the kitchen. Elizabeth's head snaps up and she squints towards the doorway, a lion who's picked up the scent of something. She's trying to decide whether or not to pursue it.

"Did you say spell?" you say feeling stronger by the minute.

She glances down at you and says wryly, "What? Don't I have sorceress written on my forehead?" You have to smile.

The phone rings again urgently. She squeezes your shoulder. "Will you excuse me for just a moment? Something tells me I need to answer this." She looks deep into your eyes as though she can read the answer for herself.

"Yes. I feel better. I promise," you say. Are you really this chosen girl that Emma predicted, the one they've been waiting for all along?

Elizabeth comes back, her face is pale with worry and she's tapping her lips with her fingertips. She can barely speak. "That was Edith Cadwell. We have to get you home. Chloe LaFleur is gone."

"Gone?!" you cry, bolting upright. "What do you mean, gone?"

"Kidnapped, possibly? Or lost?" Elizabeth shakes her head. "Or something worse."

Elizabeth looks at you with concern.

"There are six girls like you in your class. There's a reason we've brought you here, and many reasons we are protecting you. Chloe is one of you, and now she has disappeared."

COMING IN OCTOBER :

FABULOUS TERRIBLE, The Adventures of You: Chloe

a note about the font

The typeface of this book is Kandal, a font created by Mark Simonson in 1994. It is named for the town of Kandal, Norway and rhymes with the word "bundle."

This book is printed on Enviro 100, a paper created in Quebec that is 100% recycled.

author biography

Sophie Talbot attended a school much like Trumbull Woodhouse, where she was president of her Sixth Form class.

credits:

Special thanks to the many talented people who contributed to FABULOUS TERRIBLE:

Shannon Gilligan, Publisher,
who made this book possible in every way.

And to: Melissa Bounty for editorial guidance. Dot Greene of Greene Dot Design for inspiring the beautiful cover design and for the Trumbull Woodhouse school seal design. Stacey Boyd of Big Eyedea Design for the outstanding interior design and layout. Cait Close and Kris Town for proofreading and early brainstorming. Chriss Mitchell for sales consultation and proofreading. Deborah Sloan for marketing consultation. Jessica Stites for technology ideas. Emma Bounty, Jessica Krupa, and Jessica DiNapoli for many great cover shots. Emma Levin, Tessa Rose and Becky Silvers from Kingswood-Oxford School for early input.

And finally: To R. A. Montgomery, the original brains behind *"The Adventures of You."*